Praise for *The Second Mrs. Hockaday*

An Indie Next Pick
A LibraryReads Selection

"Suspenseful and satisfying."   —*People*

"Susan Rivers sets this spellbinding, haunting human drama against the backdrop of the Civil War. Told through exquisitely crafted letters and diary entries, the delicious pacing leads to revelations both intriguing and unnerving. I was sorry to reach the end of this stunning debut."

—Diane Chamberlain, author of *The Silent Sister*

"Mesmerizing . . . [Rivers's] masterful prose captures the nuances of Southern mid-19th century diction. Each patiently unspooled revelation feels organic, urgent and essential to its form. Placidia's voice is penetrating and her observations about the singular truths of war are vivid and illuminating."

—*The Atlanta Journal-Constitution*

"This page-turner, set in the Civil War South, is meticulously researched and beautifully written."   —*Woman's Day*

"Spellbinding."   —*The Charlotte Observer*

"Brilliant . . . As the novel develops, Rivers intensifies the mystery and suspense even as she portrays the reality of how the inno-cent bride became the determined woman struggling to survive as her world is all but destroyed. Rivers accomplishes all of this by expertly crafting an unusual epistolary novel. Rivers' deft development of the mystery keeps you reading; her portrayal of life in the South Carolina hills when the men were away at war makes the story even more powerful."

—*Greensboro (NC) News and Record*

"The psychological and physical tolls of war, especially on women, come alive in Rivers' novel in the piteous yet gritty woman who is the second Mrs. Hockaday."   —*The Roanoke (VA) Times*

"With language evocative of the South ('craggy as a shagbark stump') and taut, almost unbearable suspense, dramatized by characters readers will swear they know, this galvanizing historical portrait of courage, determination, and abiding love mesmerizes and shocks. Similar in tone and descriptive flow to Charles Frazier's *Cold Mountain* and with the compelling narratives found in Robert Hicks' *The Widow of the South*."

—*Booklist*, starred review

"Rivers is a promising talent and an adroit storyteller. Hopefully, this won't be her only foray into fiction. A compulsively readable work that takes on the legacy of slavery in the United States, the struggles specific to women, and the possibilities for empathy and forgiveness."   —*Kirkus Reviews*

"A stirring Civil War–era version of *The Scarlet Letter*. Told through gripping, suspenseful letters, court documents, and diary entries, Rivers's story spans three decades to show the rippling effects of buried secrets, when the Hockadays and future generations must learn to overcome the damage this secret and the war have done to all the families involved."   —*Publishers Weekly*

"With *The Second Mrs. Hockaday*, Susan Rivers viscerally evokes a bygone era without sentimentality. Her deeply sympathetic characters cope with the hard truths of slavery and war, maintaining their humanity and capability for redemption throughout. A thoroughly engrossing and affecting read."
                    —Alice LaPlante, author of *A Circle of Wives*

"In *The Second Mrs. Hockaday*, Rivers gives readers an illuminating glimpse into a part of our country's past that still has repercussions in the present."   —*BookPage*

"Fans of Geraldine Brooks's *Year of Wonders* and Sarah Blake's *The Postmistress* will enjoy this solid historical novel, which is also a good choice for book clubs, as Dia's motivations for her actions will yield great discussions."   —*Library Journal*

"Rivers has masterfully told a story of the loss of human innocence as well as the forgiveness and understanding it takes to survive in a cold and unfair world. Each entry in the novel is captivating, pulling at the reader's heartstrings with moments of bliss and heartbreak, while also teasing them with small doses of details with the promise of a satisfying reveal. Rivers shows us a world past that rings true to the readers of today, a world in which circumstances are more than they first appear, the ties of loyalty are strong, and all acts of courage are great — no matter the size."   —*The Jackson (MS) Clarion-Ledger*

"Lyrically and believably written . . . The dialogue, as one might expect from a playwright, is flawless . . . The book burns brightly because Rivers has created in her young heroine a beacon of innate courage and moral clarity which challenges us all to locate these traits in ourselves."   —*Chapter 16*

"A compulsively readable debut novel about love by an accomplished playwright. Nobody else can write an unputdownable historical and mystery novel at the same time like Rivers."
                                          —*The Washington BookReview*

"A powerful story of the depths to which the human spirit can sink and still be able to survive."   —*Charleston Currents*

"A provocative, fascinating novel that reveals much about human nature—the will to survive is almost unbreakable—and about the devastations of war on the home front . . . Revealing, well written and intriguing . . . A remarkable journey, with characters who will live long in your mind."   —*Salisbury (NC) Post*

"I gobbled this book up in one in luscious sitting, wishing I could slow down and savor the prose but too eager to find out what happened. Rivers is an unflinching truth teller. Her characters are deeply human, drawn with compassion and exquisite detail."
                                          —Hillary Jordan, author of *Mudbound*

THE

SECOND

MRS.

HOCKADAY

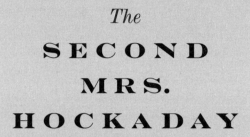

The

SECOND
MRS.
HOCKADAY

.....

Susan Rivers

.....

ALGONQUIN BOOKS

OF CHAPEL HILL

2017

Published by
Algonquin Books of Chapel Hill
Post Office Box 2225
Chapel Hill, North Carolina 27515-2225

a division of Workman Publishing
225 Varick Street
New York, New York 10014

First paperback edition, Algonquin Books of Chapel Hill, November 2017.
First published in hardcover by Algonquin Books of Chapel Hill in January 2017.
Printed in the United States of America.
Published simultaneously in Canada by
Thomas Allen & Son Limited.

Design by Barbara M. Bachman

Quotations from Marcus Aurelius's *The Emperor's Handbook* reprinted
with the permission of Scribner, a Division of Simon & Schuster, Inc., from
The Emperor's Handbook: A New Translation of the Meditations by Marcus Aurelius,
translated by C. Scot Hicks and David V. Hicks. Copyright © 2002 by
C. Scot Hicks and David V. Hicks. All rights reserved.

Passages from Virgil's *The Aeneid* reprinted with the permission of Little,
Brown and Company from *Mythology* by Edith Hamilton, translated portions
of the Aeneid by Virgil. Copyright © 1942 by Edith Hamilton.

This is a work of fiction. While, as in all fiction,
the literary perceptions and insights are based on experience,
all names, characters, places, and incidents either are
products of the author's imagination or are used fictitiously.

LIBRARY OF CONGRESS
CATALOGING-IN-PUBLICATION DATA
Names: Rivers, Susan, [date] author.
Title: The second Mrs. Hockaday : a novel / by Susan Rivers.
Description: First edition. | Chapel Hill, North Carolina : Algonquin Books
of Chapel Hill, 2016.
Identifiers: LCCN 2016007696 | ISBN 9781616205812 (hardcover)
Subjects: LCSH: Adultery—Fiction. | Married women—Fiction. | Fugitive
slaves—South Carolina—Fiction. | South Carolina—History—Civil War,
1861–1865—Fiction. | LCGFT: Historical fiction.
Classification: LCC PS3618.I859 S43 2016 | DDC 813/.6—dc23
LC record available at https://lccn.loc.gov/2016007696

ISBN 978-1-61620-736-6 (paperback)

10 9 8 7 6 5 4 3 2

to Frederick and Lily
the soil and the sun

Know that in time those things toward
which we move come to be.

—MARCUS AURELIUS,
BOOK SIX, *The Emperor's Handbook*,
TRANSLATED BY
C. SCOT HICKS AND DAVID V. HICKS

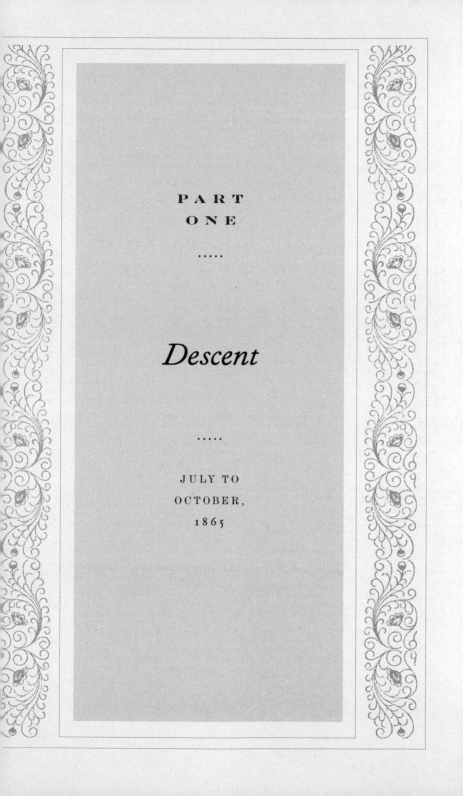

PART
ONE

.....

Descent

.....

JULY TO
OCTOBER,
1865

July 20, 1865

Dearest Mildred,

On my deathbed I shall remember that April day if I remember anything at all. I rode Banjo the yearling all the
way to the river and back because Father said she wasn't
broken yet for any but the Devil to ride and I said the
Devil and your daughter, put the saddle on. Ephraim's
eyes got wide and he went to find Abner—Ephraim always was scared witless of green horses. Abner got her
saddled and said watch out for the geese Miss P., don't run
'em flat like last time and I said more food for the wedding
guests tomorrow and tore out of the yard with Father's
laughter booming. It was such good medicine.

The sun had slipped behind the ridge when I walked
Banjo home and the darkness was creeping upwards with
its cool breath and sugar scents. I smelled cigar smoke
from the arbor. The horse walked straight there and
dropped her head, cropping the new shoots on the scup-
pernong and ignoring me because she knew her work was
done. Father ducked out of the arbor followed by a thin,
tall man with a wind-burned face as craggy as a shagbark stump. He wore an officer's uniform not very clean
and the hair slipping over his eyes was too long for good
society.

Did you wear her down? Father asked, feeling Banjo's neck for sweat, and I answered she's too gentle for the Devil anyhow not knowing why I should be bragging for a stranger's benefit. The soldier didn't smile but the way his dark eyes fixed on me made my skin stand away from my body in the oddest way. This is Major Hockaday, my father told me. He bought a mule from me today. Major, this is my daughter Placidia.

The daughter being married tomorrow? the soldier asked, disbelieving. He hadn't taken his eyes off me. I thought about how wild and dirty I must look after galloping through rough country since lunchtime and I regretted not going straight to the barn but Father shook his head and clarified that Agnes the bride was his second wife Carthene's child and did not live with us at Valois.

What mule did you buy? I asked so I could keep the major talking and when neither man answered I said Brownie with the star on her forehead? The major shook his head slowly once puffing on his long cigar do you advise that? he asked with his face all in shadow except when the embers lit up his cheeks and eyebrows and I shook my head slowly not knowing how I found the brass to say no sir we call her Brownie for she is always in the rear. Law, Mildred, it was true satisfaction to make my father laugh and he laughed more that spring than he ever laughed again. But the stranger didn't make a noise. I could barely see his face by now but his eyes were still turned up to me and they were shining with something I did not understand. Sadie, he said. The big girl built like a mountain. That's the one I bought.

Father said Major are you staying in Traveler's Joy tonight? If you don't have to rush back to Holland Creek I'd be honored if you would be our guest at the wedding in the morning. We cannot do fancy anymore but we can promise you a decent meal and quality tobacco before you return to the 13th.

He agreed. He and my father talked some more while Banjo chewed the vines and snorted. Just as I flicked the reins to start her towards the barn, the major said to Father, not to me, Placidia, that's an unusual name. For a girl who rides halfway to Georgia in a day. My father sighed. Her dear mother named her. In that respect I fear I failed to keep my parting promises.

I walked Banjo to the barn where I was glad of Abner's company as we brushed and fed and settled her. Something had changed but I did not know what it was. All I knew was that I could not seem to swallow. And the curry brush kept jumping out of my hand.

...

DOCTOR GORDON WROTE TO me saying I should not be in jail more than another day or two. He is riding over from Glenn Springs in that time and is bringing the entire amount of my bond which is not going to please some people. Write to me at Mrs. Strickland's the address enclosed she is Dr. Gordon's widowed sister. Please send me some writing paper—I do not like to ask Dr. Gordon when he is extending himself so much already. And Millie if you can possibly spare it I would greatly appreciate the loan of a dress and some essential linen as I had to come away with just the clothes on my back and I cannot return to Holland Creek nor even write to him to send me anything.

Your affectionate cousin,
Placidia

248 East Queen Street,

PENDLETON,
SOUTH CAROLINA

July 28, 1865

Dear Cousin Dia,

I have been desolate since receiving the letter from your stepsister Agnes relating the events that transpired at Holland Creek and explaining the grievance lodged against you by one whom I would never have expected to utter a critical word in reference to you. I could not have believed it if you had not written to me in your hand and confirmed the proceedings as well as the events that precipitated them. I implored you for an explanation because I badly want to defend you to your detractors with a rational argument supported by evidence. In response you sent me a narrative about your early acquaintance with Major Hockaday that will not suit my purpose. Can you not confide in your closest female relation, Placidia? Can you not give me ammunition to fire back at the self-righteous gossips who claim to know your motives almost as intimately as they appear to know the details of your crime? Women like to think the worst of women more admired than they, and I fear the sexes are lining up on opposite sides of public opinion in this matter, with women in our circle condemning you for wild iniquities and men mumbling about the war having left women unregulated and unprotected. Your stepmother says you won't tell anyone what happened and that is why there is so much sentiment against you because they say you are protecting some man who has proven himself highly unworthy when you would not protect a blameless infant you carried for nine months.

Dearest girl: in trying to gather as much positive information as I may uncover from this remove, I was introduced to a Mrs. Borders here in Pendleton who fled Winnsboro ahead of the federals. This respectable lady knows the widowed doctor upon whose hospitality and capable assistance you currently depend. She assures me that Dr. Gordon and Mrs. Strickland enjoy a reputation that is beyond reproach. I would expect no less, knowing how far you have obligated yourself to them; however, I confess to feeling no small concern on your behalf, Placidia, because I know you to be a creature of almost Edenic innocence, composed of rather too many parts enthusiasm in proportion to your share of apprehension, somewhat akin to Eve before she tasted the apple (or even beheld the tree, more precisely . . .) I do not intend this as a criticism but merely as a caution from one who loves you unreservedly. I have never spoken against your attachment to "Adam," nor have I made any judgment as to the precipitous nature of that union (in truth, I had no chance), but any objective view of your current catastrophe must concede that you rush into close associations with your heart galloping forward while your head lags behind, blinded by dust and distance.

You can be certain that in concerning myself with your affairs I am trying to help you resolve them happily and remind you of the benefits you derive from doing so.

"The Lord is my portion, saith my soul; therefore will I
hope in him."

...

(MORNING OF THE NEXT day, on a practical note . . .) I
was forced to leave most of my dresses in Cheraw when
we fled ahead of the army in late February, and while I
cannot imagine what use Sherman's bluecoats had for a
cupboard full of mourning-wear (although I wished their
women use of it, quite fervently), my neighbors reported
that my house was entirely plundered down to the door-
knobs, with every scrap of clothing, crystal, and cutlery
carted off. General Hardee bolted ahead of the enemy
with indecent haste, I am told, leaving the warehouses
filled with Charleston's treasures, the armory packed with
cannon, and his wounded soldiers groaning for mercy
in Town Hall. Viewing my losses in this context I could
hardly bemoan a few claret glasses, and as word made its
way to us of the sufferings endured by our countrymen
in Columbia, Camden, and Winnsboro (from whence
Mrs. Borders relates a story too horrific in its details to
be apochryphal: of how Geary's bummers dragged the
organ from the Episcopal Church as it burned and played
drinking songs upon it, but not satisfied with that enter-
tainment, dug up a freshly interred coffin from the churchyard, tore off the lid, and set the coffin on end so that the
corpse could better view their minstrel show! . . .) I realized how fortunate it was that my house was not torched,
and Cheraw along with it. And our dead, while inevitably
spinning in their graves, were at least spared desecration.

The only dress I brought along to Pendleton which

might suit is an old delaine I wore when I was staying in at home and felt my spirits too depressed to put on crêpe. I will send it to you by way of my father-in-law when he travels through Holland County next week on his way to the coast. It has bishop sleeves and the cloth was fawn when new with a pattern of roses and ivy in wreaths. It was let out when my measurements increased (Baby Roe) and altered again when she was weaned and I must warn you not to allow your expectations to rise too high for although its quality was once quite good the dress has been mended many times and has absorbed every fluid an infant with a healthy appetite can produce but I am glad you are letting me take some positive action on your behalf at last, no matter how incidental. Also I will enclose a yoked chemise and some other necessaries.

Ever yours,
Mildred

3982 Glenn Springs Road,

GLENN SPRINGS,
SOUTH CAROLINA

August 10, 1865

Dear Mildred,

I can scarcely convey the contrast between my present
accommodations at Dr. Gordon's house and the austere
quarters I occupied in the Holland County Jail, so I will
not attempt it, except to tell you that Glenn Springs is a
perfect Arcadia and the Gordons' house is the handsomest
cottage on the street. In fact, I haven't acquainted myself
with the town beyond what I can see of it from the doctor's fence-line; he says I may walk up the road to Cates'
store and the post office if I wish because no one in this
county will know that I am a notorious character from
a neighboring district. However, I am wary of gossips,
knowing the damage they can do, and content myself
with reading in the doctor's excellent library, visiting with
Mrs. Strickland, and loitering around the stable, where
the Gordons' groom endures me with patient goodwill.
His grandson sometimes joins him there, a watchful child
about Charlie's age, who tolerates my poor aptitude for
clapping games but easily accepts my preference for small
boys and horses over grown-up companions. Young
Noah and I find comfort in sharing summer apples and
confidences with the carriage horses; one of them is very
like Banjo, and I spoil her. There was no opportunity to
ask my husband what became of my filly, but I can well

imagine her fate, knowing how few soldiers from the regiment survived the butchery at the Wilderness and the Bloody Angle. I tell myself it is unseemly to mourn a horse, considering.

Millie, I grow ashamed of myself when I consider the extent to which *you* have been tested by this war, demonstrating calmness and courage when no one would blame you for a full loss of composure. I know you maintain it for your daughter's sake. Try to understand, then, that my circumspection is all I currently possess—so long as I can fortify it—to protect those I love and shield others to whom I am wholly indebted, including Dr. Gordon and his sister.

I know you are trying to aid me, and I am grateful for the dress which if it has been utilized as fully as you say will serve me honorably, so I entrust you with the pieces of my story, if not the whole cloth. You are entirely correct in describing me as a person guided too much by her heart; as I grow older I understand that such impulses too often lead me into conflict with the heart's desires of others, discovering the topography of the landscape into which I have blundered too late to regain my footing. I am endeavoring to amend that now, before my situation becomes hopeless, but what I cannot excise from my mind is the conviction that I am guided by Destiny—or, what you would call Providence—at the most harrowing intersections of my life. What I can state without prevarication is that my current destiny was charted over the course of two short days in April '63. And wasn't it you, dear Cousin, who once told me that "life is all about the leaps"? You said that is why you married Arthur when you were only eighteen, and when he was felled at Sharps-burg you mourned him but you continued to feel blessed, because you said those six months you shared with him were the best months of your life and his also, as he told you so often. You had Baby Roe to wake up for every day and you would never have known her or been favored by Mr. Jones's affections if you had not taken that huge leap when everyone was advising caution and telling you to see what assurances life would offer before you took a step in any direction. Did you not tell me that? Something like that was happening to me the evening I rode Banjo back from the river and smelled the cigar smoke in the arbor. I recognized that I had been waiting for my life to begin and all of a sudden it bolted forward so fast I could barely hang on.

The next morning I was up before dawn because the house had never really quieted down the night before. Nerissa and Carthene were barricaded in Carthene's room with Agnes, packing her bridal trousseau and getting her dressed, so I helped Mercy in the kitchen, baking Con-federate pound cake out of bolted cornmeal. I wish you had been able to ride over, Millie, because that was the last time Father and I and Aunt Florie and the rest of the fam-ily were all together except for you and Roe but I know there is not much you can do when a baby is sick except to exercise the patience of a saint which is what you are.

The cousins from Orangeburg arrived late and brought cider. Agnes's brother Nolan and their paternal grand-mother Mrs. Oglesby, and Miss Katherine Cooper,

Agnes's close companion from Miss Murden's Seminary for Young Ladies, came along from Charleston by way of Mrs. Oglesby's townhome in Columbia, riding in her carriage with two strong servants alongside to protect the horses. I heard Miss Cooper greet my stepmother warmly but then she turned aside and complained more quietly to Agnes that Nolan had been quite fresh with her all the way from Blanding Street, and out of deafness or indifference Mrs. Oglesby made no move to inhibit him. I was glad Nolan lived with his father's people in Charleston and rarely came to Valois since it fell far short of his standards. He presumed liberties with the fairer sex yet always did so disdainfully, as if to say that he was only carrying on so out of a surfeit of boredom and that his teasing a lady to tears was merely intended as a temporary distraction.

When Rev. Poteat was announced and the wedding was about to start I rushed out of the kitchen slapping cornmeal off my skirts and nearly collided with the major. I hardly recognized him. He had bathed and shaved and changed into civilian clothes he must have borrowed because the sleeves were a little short and the collar frayed. Without the uniform he seemed younger although in the sunlit parlor I could make out a scar on his throat angling up behind his left ear that made me think of Blackbeard. He seemed less sure of himself in this setting and in these clothes and I liked that too.

Miss Placidia, he said in his rough voice. You break horses. You bake. Is there anything you cannot do? I cannot dance, I answered, though it is not for lack of trying. You shall dance with me, he said, tugging at his short cuffs. No one will notice your deficiencies because they will be entirely focused on my ghastly lack of grace.

How he knew there would be dancing is still a mystery to me, as Floyd Parris had hired the two musicians as a wedding present for Agnes and it was a surprise to everyone except Floyd and Major Hockaday when the fiddler and the mandolin player walked out on the piazza after the bride and groom were joined and launched into a lively rendition of "The Southern Soldier Boy." They must have played the tune ten times that day and into the night and everyone danced including Father and Auntie F.

At some point Nolan and a pair of my male cousins, having imbibed too large a portion of cider, were popping in and out of the pantry to Mercy's displeasure in search of hardier comestibles than the table provided. I was coming along the back hallway to shoo them off when I overheard the younger cousin say to Nolan I hear you petted a pretty Kitty on the long ride to Traveler's Joy and the older cousin jumped in saying petted her I heard but he didn't make her purr. I paused to hear what Nolan would reply. Katherine is a nice enough old maid, he said, but that sassy stepsister of mine gets me harder than Chinese arithmetic.

I didn't know exactly what he meant but I knew it was disgusting because the cousins brayed like donkeys. If I'm being honest I felt a little flutter of vanity in the depths of my imperfect character and again I can't say why. Everything about those two days when the major came to buy a mule and Agnes married Floyd Parris was confusing and exciting and frightening. I was not quite myself and if I'm being honest I never found my way back to the girl I used to be.

Note: must stop here for now as Mrs. Strickland has come in. I promised to read to her this afternoon because she is nearly blind. She is an elderly lady and also hard of hearing so I begin to wonder if she knows who I am.

August 11, 1865

I didn't finish telling you about the wedding and how I danced with Major Hockaday three waltzes. His hands were calloused and he held me at a distance in the way Abner holds a fresh coonskin—like he was fixing to nail me to a shed before the smell made his eyes water. He didn't look at me the way he had the day before—he seemed to be avoiding my face. I asked him his Christian name and he had to mull it over. He finally told me it was a Welsh name he had never been able to spell nor had anyone else so he called himself "Griff." He was telling the truth when he said he was a poor dancer and he was so tall I had to tilt my head back to see his jaw and his Adam's apple while we danced. But as the music ended he guided me into the alcove in the dining room where his left hand slid down my back while his right hand pulled me to his side. I stumbled. He smoothly righted me with his hands on my waist. Didn't I tell you I was clumsy, I said, and I must have been blushing because I fancied my hair was on fire. Not a bit, he said, fixing his eyes on mine at last. Don't forget I've seen you ride a pony.

...

SOMETHING HAPPENED THAT NIGHT I wish I could forget. The musicians played and people danced until sundown. Father and Carthene toasted the couple with eggnog before they left in Floyd's carriage for Laurens, with my stepbrother and his inebriated companions serenading them. As soon as the bride and groom departed and the formalities were dispensed with my stepmother took Nolan aside and tried to talk him into behaving but it only wound him up. He declared with much hilarity that he and the boys were in the mood to go coon hunting and Father told him to wait until daylight and not to go into the brush now else he'd destroy his white flannel trousers and the waistcoat his mother had embroidered. The major seemed alert to Nolan's precipitate mood and asked Father quietly if he could be of any assistance settling the lads but Father was embarrassed by the fuss and asked Aunt Florie to play the piano.

Most of us moved into the back parlor where my mother's piano stood by the window and we sat in the chairs and on the ottomans there while the little boys, Cyrus and Tony, lit the candles. I sat with Miss Cooper and conversed with her for half an hour about the assault on Charleston Harbor by the Federals' ironclads which proved to be all bark and no bite and she says people there are becoming so conditioned to cannon-fire that no one at her table was alarmed enough to suspend dinner. At one point she asked me if Major Hockaday was kin and her curiosity flustered me so that I stumbled over the words telling her he was only here buying a mule. The way she cast her gaze across the parlor to the doorway made me

turn my head to follow her eyes. The major stood against
the pillar with his arms crossed, watching my aunt at the
piano, but there was no concealing the thread of attention
that seemed to originate in his chest and stretch across
the room to the hollow space at the base of my throat. It
might as well have been a magnetic cord, or the fuse on a
firework, snapping with sparks. Whatever his intention,
Miss Cooper whispered in my ear, I don't believe the mule
is half of it.

But that's not the part I wish to forget. Aunt Florie
concluded the final movement of the Schubert sonata and
respectful silence met the last resounding chord of music.
Into that silence our guests relaxed and sighed, turning to
one another to comment on the fine quality of my aunt's
musicianship. That's when one or two and then more of
them noticed Nolan stepping into the room to sweep up
an unclaimed cup of eggnog. What we all perceived in the
pool of lamplight that illuminated him was how vividly his
costume had been altered. The knees of his white trousers
were stained red with dirt.

Excepting Major Hockaday, the few men in attendance
at the wedding had slipped out of the room by this time,
following Father into his study where the windows would
be open to the cooling air and bottles of his Tennessee
whiskey would be brought out. I thanked the Creator that
my father was not there to see his stepson's *déshabillé*. My
stepmother's face was the color of chalk and her red mouth
had gone rigid, but she said nothing to Nolan, nor did any
other lady in the room, including me. What could be said?
Young Master Oglesby had clearly gone "hunting" out in

the dark beyond the tea olives, in the small white building where our house servants lived or in the larger cabins down the hill where the smoke from the cooking pots of six families rose into the willow oaks. Sitting in our candle-lit room enjoying the *Sonata in A Major* we did not rebuke him for it. We looked away.

The major stepped forward and wrapped one long arm around Nolan's shoulders while lifting the cup out of his hand. Let's get something stronger, bonny boy. I know where to find it.

Before Nolan could protest he was marched out of the parlor across the hall and out the front entrance. The door's slam echoed up the stairs. Father emerged from the study, looking to me. Is everything satisfactory? he asked our guests, eyeing the carpet turned up in the hall. The women gave him thin smiles, reaching for their wraps. He questioned Carthene with his eyes but she wouldn't look at him. Or me. She went to the parlor window and peered outside, searching the shadows for her son. I watched her, thinking: I hope she fails to find him before my major finishes his catechism.

...

THE NEXT DAY I woke feeling almost normal again in my head and my heart, but as I walked to the stable to visit the horses I was bothered by fragments of dreams so confusing I couldn't have told Abner if I'd had good dreams or bad. Abner was shoveling out the stalls with a face clouded by care. I should have asked him what the matter was, but I was so young still, Millie, and when we're young we're selfish and we only care about ourselves. I looked past Abner and was shocked to see a big gray mule nudging the hay in her box. Has the soldier left Sadie behind, I asked him and I had to repeat it because my voice cracked the first time.

Mr. Fincher says I'm to tell you to go on in the house directly, Abner told me, and don't mess with the livestock before doing so. He says you're to have clean hands and face. Abner didn't seem abashed at having to scold.

The doors were closed to the front parlor, a troubling sign. I tried to tiptoe across the hall to the stairs but my father parted the doors and looked out, frowning. Come in, Placidia. We're waiting. I stepped into the shadowy room with my hand planted on my chest to stop my heart from jumping out but the major wasn't there. Carthene frowned at me from the divan.

I've received an offer of marriage on your behalf, does that surprise you? My father searched my face. I nodded. It surprised me too. Gryffth Hockaday has been away since Pocataligo—he's seen some of the bloodiest fighting this bloody war has to offer and has been promoted twice. This trip was the first leave he's had in nearly a year and he took it because his wife died at Holland Creek of typhoid fever. The news didn't reach him until two months after she died, and by then his baby boy was doing poorly. He arrived home in time to find a doctor for the child and get his farm in better order—that's what the mule is all about. His regiment needs him—they're on the move soon from their winter camp in Virginia. However, he's got it in his head—and this wasn't the plan until he laid eyes on you, he informs me—that he can't go back to Lee's army until he's gambled his heart on winning something worth coming home to. He wants that something to be you.

It was so silent in the parlor that the air had a weighty presence all its own. I was afraid to draw it in. I'm to be a mother, I said at last, and Carthene made a noise of disapprobation. My father put his hand on her shoulder, whether to quiet her or reassure her I couldn't tell.

Only if you choose to be, he said. Gryffth Hockaday is respected in Holland County, where we share some relations. He's a competent farmer with 300 acres, about half of it cleared and planted. He tells me that he plans to breed racehorses when the war is over, and I've no doubt he's got the talent for that. But we need not feel obligated to play so crucial a role in fulfilling this man's dreams. I know him a little. You, not at all. You will have your own plans and dreams when you get older, Placidia. And there is no doubt in my mind that you will have other offers.

He's not suitable, Carthene declared. She was clearly in a bad humor: every inch of her asserted it, from her untidy hair to the creases in her wrapper. He's not well-placed. Not like the Oglesbys. The Finchers. Not like Floyd Parris.

If I thought the man disreputable, Father said, I wouldn't part with my mule, much less my only child.

His mother's family ran a livery stable, Carthene continued. His grandfather was a coal miner!

His grandfather is not wooing my daughter, Father snapped, and I was gratified by this display of temper, so rare for my father, in support of my suitor.

In any case, he's too old for her, Carthene complained,

and I understood that her poor disposition arose out of
the timing of the soldier's proposal, as if he and I had con-
spired to steal her daughter's thunder .

Father conceded this point soberly. He's thirty-two
years old, he said to me. He's nearly twice your age. Marriage lasts a long time. Wouldn't you be happier with a
young man closer to you in years?

I didn't know how to answer him. I thought of your
dear husband, Millie, so lively and smart, cut down in a
cornfield on his twentieth birthday. I thought of all the
other young men who'd fallen at Shiloh and Antietam and
all the county boys who were, at that moment, fighting
for their lives in typhoid wards in Staunton or starving in
Camp Douglas or battling the enemy in Virginia, Tennessee, Arkansas, Kentucky. I shook my head but I couldn't
speak. Where was happiness to be found in a country that
sacrifices its bravest and best?

Father abruptly stepped forward and took my hand. He
asked Carthene to have Mercy serve coffee and biscuits
in the parlor in half an hour, leading me out the back hall.
He said, I've asked your major to wait in the study where
he can read the Richmond papers. The way he said "your
major" surprised me, even though I already thought of
Hockaday that way. I worried that Father held me responsible for this disruptive turn of events.

Are you angry, Daddy, I asked him. His face softened.
You haven't called me that in years.

We pushed through the gate into the little kitchen
garden that hugged the south wall of the house. This
had always been our place for secrets. The first time he

brought me here I barely stood as tall as his belt buckle.
He gave me a radish to nibble and told me that my mother
was dead. Now as we passed under the pea trellis I spied
Nerissa setting onions. She wore a kerchief bound tightly
to her head and one side of her face was bruised. The
troubled look in her eyes was the same one I had seen on
Abner's face in the stable that morning. Remembering
that Abner was sweet on Nerissa, and reminding myself
of Nolan Oglesby's transgressions the night before, I felt a
pang of guilty dread on behalf of them.

Have you hurt yourself, Nerissa, Father asked as we
approached. She hesitated, glancing quickly at me. No
Master Fincher. It's healing. She gathered the unplanted
onions and left.

Cabbages grew in rows beside the path. I watched bees
hovering above the strawberry blossoms. I'm not angry at
you, Daughter, he said at last. I'm frustrated. I knew this
day was coming, but I fooled myself that I had plenty of
time yet. There is never enough time. Certainly not when
a war is on. Here he paused, looking over his shoulder
into the sunny yard. He pulled me deeper into the garden
where the fig's branches closed over us. Leaf buds the size
of peas were sprouting on the long spurs, and they were so
intensely green that I could have bitten them off and eaten
them.

Father said, I paid a call on a doctor in Mobile when
I went downriver this winter. A specialist I'd been told
could help me with my headaches. He gave me some
powders and said I should plan for the short term, not
the long.

I clenched his hand, but he was staring fixedly at a sparrow plucking a piece of twine in the arbor.

I want to see you well taken care of when I'm gone, Dia. In service of that desire, I am asking you to do the impossible. I am asking you to make a decision that will shape the rest of your life. And you must make your choice in very little time with almost no information. Can you do that?

I bent down and closed my hand over the cluster of berry blossoms, trapping a honeybee. I told myself if the bee stings me I won't marry anyone. I'll stay and care for Father and grow old in the only home I've known. I waited, while the bee buzzed and bounced against my palm, so persistently I imagined it might be tapping out a message on my skin. He said what do you say, Placidia?

I said I want to see the major. I opened my hand and the bee rose dizzily out of the garden.

...

THE REVEREND WAS CALLED back and the ham was served again. I brushed the cornmeal off my blue taffeta, since it was the best dress I owned, and Nerissa picked me a bouquet of jonquils. Major Hockaday had donned his uniform again, telling me it would keep us safer on our way home, and when he said "home" and I understood that this was a place I had never seen in a county where I had never been, I felt my insides cramp.

He wouldn't touch me while we were all in the parlor together and Poteat was saying the words. But after the ceremony he reached for my hand and clasped it tightly. He whispered that he had a good feeling about us, that we were going to survive the war and make strong children together. When he whispered in my ear about making children I wanted to curl my whole body into his warm dry hand and stay there forever. But there was so little time. He said we had to get to Holland Creek before nightfall and it was a long ride.

Father made a gift of Banjo to us although I knew he could hardly spare her. He tried to return Sadie's price to Hockaday as well, but my husband refused. He accepted the loan of Abner, telling Father and Carthene that he had a strong girl and an old woman back at Holland Creek who would help me with the child and the household. Father reminded me that Agnes and Floyd were twelve miles from where we'd be living, that he'd already written a letter to Floyd asking him and his wife to look in on me later that spring. Then Hockaday settled me in the carriage with Ephraim, who was driving us to the farm with my trunk, and climbed on his horse. I did not look back at my home. I knew I wouldn't be able to leave it if I did.

To be continued.

Faithfully yours,
Dia

INQUEST NO. 27,

HOLLAND COUNTY,
SOUTH CAROLINA

An inquest was held at the home of Major and Mrs. Gryffyth Hockaday on July 15, 1865, Coroner M. B. Upchurch conducting and Magistrate J. W. Mitchell assisting. This followed disinterment of a deceased fetus that was buried in a thicket on the banks of Holland Creek. The male infant was wrapped in a piece of knitting and placed in a sewing box or knife box. The infant was judged to be slightly undersized by the coroner but was not stillborn; given the state of decomposition, race could not be determined. The coroner estimates the infant was buried for four to six months.

Major Gryffth Hockaday age 35 sworn says, I arrived in Holland Creek after an absence of nearly two years. I was captured in battle on Squirrel Level Road outside Petersburg on September 30 1864 and confined to a Federal prison camp for officers on Johnson's Island in Ohio until my release in June 1865. Over several weeks' time I made my way home walking and occasionally obtaining rides. When I was ten miles from home I was taken on a dray hauling barrels. I fell into conversation with the driver about some of the particulars of my experience and our talk turned naturally to my destination and the wife who waited for me. This drayman seemed surprised to know that I was the husband of Mrs. Hockaday. After some reluctance to speak further on the matter he claimed to have heard all over town about this woman's reputation but refused to provide particulars. He put me out at the crossroads of the Holland Creek Road and Laurens Branch Road.

I was less than a mile from the farm of former neighbors and friends, Mister Byars and his wife, so I walked there and asked if I could stay and rest for an hour or two as I was still endeavoring to regain my strength after prison life and was also taken faint by this information about my wife. Byars kindly settled me on the porch and gave me some brandy. He was reluctant to repeat gossip being spread about Mrs. Hockaday but eventually shared what he had heard. Byars said it was generally known among the town's residents that my wife had carried a child during the summer, fall, and winter of 1864 and may have given birth to this infant at the farm, alone, in January of 1865. That child had never been seen by anyone in Holland Crossroads and was presumed dead. I had been absent from my wife since April 1863, carrying out my duties to my country while serving the 13th Regiment of South Carolina Volunteers, and despite my attempts to be furloughed for at least one reunion with her in North Carolina during that time I was prevented from doing so and therefore had not been with her at all during that period. I questioned Byars closely about whether or not Placidia had made a statement to anyone regarding the pregnancy, the child, or the child's paternity and he answered that she had not. However, he told me Floyd Parris had been frequently seen coming and going in his buggy on the Laurens Branch Road during the time this child was supposedly conceived.

I was so distressed by this information that I could not stay a moment longer on my neighbor's porch but walked the rest of the way to Holland Creek, arriving before nightfall. My wife was at home. We were both very emotional at that first meeting and I cannot adequately describe the conflicting impulses I experienced.

When I was able to speak rationally I questioned her about the rumors I had heard and she wept freely while admitting that she did birth a child who lived but a few hours. However, she did not enlighten me further. I asked her if while I was fighting in Fredericksburg, Chancellorsville, and Gettysburg, where I lost two fingers on my left hand, in the Wilderness, Spotsylvania, and in the slaughter-pens of Petersburg where we ate our horses' corn to keep from starving, if while I was absent she had transferred her affections to Floyd Parris or some other attentive man who drove a buggy. She would not reply. I asked if any man white or negro Confederate or Bluecoat had forced an encounter on her but she did not answer and continued to cry.

At that time I asked my son to be brought to me and my wife woke Charles and put him in my arms. As he had not seen me for over two years the child did not know me and was too frightened to be soothed. I left the house that night and stayed with Byars. In the morning I rode to the magistrate in town and filed a complaint against my wife for concealing the death of the issue of her body.

August 19, 1865

Dearest Mildred,

Of all the misgivings to which we women are prone, none
is more pernicious than the suspicion that we were too
easily won.

I will tell you of my earliest hours and days as a bride
and you tell me if it's the story of a fool: one so lulled by
her seventeen years of entitlement—of love and privilege
and pony rides—that she could not know how disastrously she had been prepared for life until she stepped
into the world just as it was breaking into pieces.

Two things happened on the way from Valois to Holland Creek that struck me as bad omens, and I must remind you Millie that I had no reason to expect anything
but *good* fortune at the outset.

The first event took place at midday, after we had traveled about ten miles beyond the rich river valley where I
spent my life, into a series of low hills spotted with farmland. We saw fields being plowed and others planted with
corn by field hands, with the occasional overseer waving
at us from his horse. The wagon road soon yielded to
a track that plunged through mostly uncleared woods.
We passed fewer homesteads, and as the day wore on I
longed to get down from the carriage and rest, eating
from the basket Aunt Florie had packed for us. However,

my husband insisted on continuing the journey, leading us down a cut-off he claimed would save several miles. The cut-off led through a forest of pignut trees and sassafras that closed in on the carriage and made a person feel like she could hardly draw a breath. Not even the birds were calling in that gloomy place, and all we could hear for mile after mile was Hockaday directing the horses and the pignuts cracking under the wheels.

When we finally pushed through into a patchy clearing I opened my mouth to beg my husband to pause and let us rest but he was already shouting at two figures across the clearing sitting in the rosy light of a Judas tree. The men straightened when they heard him call and seemed to consult with one another. The major called again and the tallest of them walked to us, a negro dressed well enough that I supposed he was a house servant. He reminded me of Cyrus, if Cyrus were grown, and the younger one, Tony.

Where's your permits, asked the major, you're a long way from anywhere, and the Cyrus-like youth looked at Ephraim and me in the carriage and then at Abner sitting quiet on Banjo before he said we comin' from the crossroads, sir. This young man had a face you don't forget because his eyes were blue, and there is something about blue eyes on a dark smooth face that is like nothing else— you can't look away from it. I can see you've walked a lot further than that my husband argued and I could see too that the negro's shirt was stained with sweat and the way he and his companion had been slumped beneath the tree when we broke into the clearing suggested they'd walked on foot a fair distance, although I hadn't any notion where the "crossroads" might be nor did it sound encouraging of civilization.

You're Wilkerson's lot aren't you, Hockaday continued. Yessir, said the tired man and he said it like the Wilkerson's was a place devoid of hope or happiness. We just going to the post office and took this shortcut but Mose stepped on a snake and we stopped to bind the bite. We all looked across the clearing at the younger boy sitting with his foot wrapped in a rag. Where's the mail, said Hockaday. Where's the horse. Blue Eyes looked surprised. The horse? he asked. You came on horseback, my husband told him. You heard about the Gullah soldiers down in Port Royal and you thought you might could make it there. No sir that's too far, said Blue Eyes but he sounded so tired that I could almost see his mind telling him he didn't have the strength to make up lies and he looked straight at Abner and said yessir we had a horse but the press gang stole it and they stole the mailbag too. If I don't get Mose back to Wilkerson's for doctoring he's gonna die.

My husband shook his head as if he had never seen or heard anything so pitiful. He told Blue Eyes to get the boy up on Sadie and he could walk beside. We had no lunch that day but traveled another hour to the post office at Holland Crossroads. Gryffth talked to the postmaster until he agreed to take charge of the runaways. The postmaster said he would send word to Mrs. Wilkerson to come and get them when she could—to save the snake-bit child if she had a mind to and retrieve the other one before he bolted again. I know what lesson Mrs. Wilkerson would have me school into that one, added Mr. Cowan, jerking his thumb at Blue Eyes. It's not the first time he's given her trouble. And now, you say, he has lost a horse.

Hold back on the armory, Cowan, my husband said coolly. Wait until you have heard from the lady, at least. A challenging undertone in his voice gave me to believe there was a contest of wills taking place between him and the postmaster, with the other man's prodigious girth seeming not to intimidate the major in the slightest. A few moments passed while they studied each other, Cowan's chin in the air. At last my husband pulled some coins from his pocket and laid them on the counter, saying with calm civility: give them food and water before locking them in there, man. Do that much as a Christian.

As we drove away I looked back trying to see if Cowan was going to tend to the boy's swollen foot or if I should have spoken up since I had once seen Mercy tie a cord around the ankle of a girl bit by a pilot snake and then cut the bite and paste wet charcoal on it, but my looking back seemed to aggravate the major. He said best not to be concerned with our neighbors' problems, Placidia, lest they concern themselves too much with ours. The slope of his brow warned me against arguing with him; it was clear he was unhappy about handing those negroes over to Cowan. I had much to learn.

After we had traveled another mile or two I broke the silence, saying what is the armory? My husband turned to me with a look of surprise, just as my tutor used to do when taken off-guard by the depths of my ignorance. He said there's an armory in Holland Crossroads. A market hall in Traveler's Joy. In Charleston it's the sugar house.

It's where servants are sent to be corrected. And he didn't
need to say more.

The second event took place at the farm. It was nearly
dark when we arrived at last. My knees buckled when the
major lifted me to the ground I was that fatigued, and seeing a cloud of chimney swifts fly up in the purple light
I marveled that it had only been forty-eight hours since
I'd first laid eyes on Gryffth Hockaday and here I was
with my world turned on its head. An old negro woman
came out on the porch. She was holding a dark-haired
baby who clung to her in terror when he fixed his eyes on
me. That's Sukie he said of the woman and that's my son
Charles. Why don't you go inside and get acquainted
with the child. I reached out to the baby intending to
stroke his head but he screamed like I was piercing him
with red hot knitting needles. What you called, asked
the negro woman, which I considered highly insolent.
Mrs. Hockaday, I answered, and her wide eyes told me I
had made an impression.

I went into the house but could not comprehend why
the lamps weren't lit. Where are the other servants, I
asked the woman when she followed me into the hall.
Ain't none, she said. Only them few in the field house
yonder. You're mistaken, Mother. My husband said there
was an old woman and a strong young girl to help me in
the house. I thought I saw a smile flicker across Sukie's
face, although it was dark where we stood. Oh that girl
run off once the major went to Valois cuz she hear Lincoln
sign a paper. I say it jes nonsense but Emelia hard-headed.

I was so shocked by the weight of this bad news that I

didn't know what to say. We stood in silence and in darkness regarding one another, the baby staring at me too. Far off I heard a panicked whinny. It was Banjo.

I pushed past the woman and hurried out to the barn where the major had removed the sorrel's saddle and was wrestling her by the bridle. Abner was standing at a distance and I could see on his face what that distance cost him. When he saw me come in he gave a little shake of his head to warn me off. My husband was cursing my horse with words I couldn't have invented on my most imaginative day. He had thrown his frock coat on the ground and was trying to back the filly into a stall but Banjo was fighting him hard. The major raised a riding crop.

She won't be backed in, I shouted at him. She must see where she's being led!

He cut a look at me, the crop suspended as he struggled to hold her. Abner looked at me too, his face distorted by tension. It was as if I had interrupted a performance that my husband was weary of playing and my servant uncomfortable with watching, but in which they both persisted through some misplaced sense of duty. I suddenly felt impatient with everyone, Banjo included. I stepped forward and took the bridle out of my husband's hand, keeping my shoulder pressed to the pony's ribs while I led her out of the stall, circled Hockaday, and walked back in, Banjo snorting her relief. I couldn't look at Abner as I called to him over the stall door—I didn't want to see his disapproval. Abner replaced me in the stall and dealt with Banjo's tack as I retrieved my husband's coat and dusted it off.

Gryffth had tossed the crop down. Now he donned his

coat, not taking his eyes off my face. I had no choice but
to return his gaze, which was as hard as flint. The feeling I
had been gripped by at Valois of knowing this man on an
intimate level receded, leaving me with only faith and fear
in equal measure.

Are you angry, I asked. He gave a brisk shake of his
head, but something unspoken remained constricted in
his face. Not thinking (again), but noting that Abner
was occupied with Banjo out of earshot and that we were
otherwise alone in the barn, I touched my fingertips to his
temple where a vein throbbed. I whispered: Can't I help
you set aside this war?

My husband took my fingers in his. He started to speak
but stopped himself. Instead of squandering on words
whatever intense condition gripped his spirit at that moment, he conveyed it in the clasping of my hand as he led
me across the yard and into the house.

*Millie: I must preface the following pages with a warning to
your modesty—recognizing that yours is still intact and worth
preserving whereas I never took much trouble to guard my own
and now it has been completely obliterated by grim events. I
would not share this narrative with any but a married woman,
but if you fear it will offend your more refined sensibilities
kindly do not read further.*

Once over the threshold I expected a discussion but
there was none—both Sukie and the tragic infant had
vanished—and the major continued leading me up the
stairs to the first spacious room off the landing. Someone
had lit a candle there and set it on the dresser. Once inside
he shut and locked the door. I heard his hat knock a wall

as he tossed it in the darkness and then, as Mercy might have said, he set for me like a pig for a tater peeling. After stripping us of our clothes (all but my corset, which is as impregnable as Fort McAllister) he laid me down on the bolster where with several vigorous, determined moves he deflowered me.

I had much time for reflection in the night that followed, with the major sleeping soundly atop me while his male *accoutrements* dried upon my thigh. (And why doesn't anyone tell us that men are fashioned in this astonishing way. Why didn't *you* tell *me*, Millie? It was not a disappointing discovery, but unexpected, yes.) Lying upstairs in the strange house I reassured myself that it was not as if Hockaday could have been satisfied with *any* woman in his bed that night. Even at the moment he buried himself fully in me there was a leaping-up of strong emotion in his sharply featured face—one of the characteristics of that nameless emotion being that he sought to meet its twin reflected in my countenance as he possessed me. I gave him what I had not out of duty but from a true avidity for the man and out of the desire to know him fully. And lest you suppose from my account that he behaved a total brute: before yielding to exhaustion my new husband kissed my face, stroked my hair, and asked me to forgive him if my first experience of connubial love had been a painful one. But Mildred, it all happened so quickly and with such disorienting intensity that when I replayed this event in my mind throughout the sleepless night that followed I could not divest myself entirely of the feeling that my new husband had stamped his dominance upon me, along with his embraces.

Waking the next morning I panicked, not knowing how I came to be in such a foreign place and not knowing in whose bed I had spent the night (nor whose blood daubed the sheet on which I lay; truly, my Aunt Florie loves me well but as a spinster she was ill-suited to prepare me for the rigors of the wedding night). The room was sizable but dark, with only one window gathering in the eastern light. An elusive scent sweetened the close air in the room, a fragrance like honey but with the fresh tang of grass underneath it. I turned on the pillow to discover one narrow jonquil slumbering there, its pearly crown identifying it as an old-fashioned flower Nerissa always called April Maid.

A clamor of birdsong sounded from the woods. I could hear men's voices in the yard below. I climbed out of bed, wrapping the coverlet about me as best I could, and went to the window to discover to what new kingdom I had been transported. The farmhouse occupied the peak of a forested ridge, with the farmyard dominated by a massive white oak and a well. It had rained during the night, and the sunlight looked newly minted where it sparkled on the roofs and in the treetops, which vibrated with that unbearably tender hue of spring green that is like the color of hope. The damp yard opened out to a smokehouse and corn crib before descending to other outbuildings, the servants' house, and a sturdy barn surrounded by pens where bullfrogs sang from the puddles. From my second-story

vantage I spied distant corners of pastureland dotted with
cattle and the raw, red gash of tilled fields, rolling gradually down to a slice of creekwater.

The effect of this setting was rougher than what I had
expected, of a vital but primary nature, as if the planter
had hacked it out of the woodland with his bare hands
not long before journeying to Valois in search of a draft
animal strong enough to help him finish the job. Energy
coursed in the trees and in the bullfrogs' song, lifting
the hawks as they sailed in circles over the streambed. It
vibrated in the red furrows and the blinding lace of dog-
wood blossoms opening to the sun, waiting to reclaim this
place from its temporary utility, to knit it back into the
fabric of the wilderness.

The voices came from two men standing at the foot of
the porch. One was a strongly built negro of mature age,
the man I would come to know as Bob, the head servant
at Holland Creek. He held a new lamb in his arms. The
second man, facing the house as he studied the lamb and
prodded it gently, was dressed in old clothes and a slouch
hat that nearly hid his face as he queried Bob. This man,
I recognized with a start, was my husband, Gryffth Rhys
Hockaday. I must have accompanied this awareness with
sudden movement, for Gryffth looked up abruptly from
under his hat. I felt silly, then, exposing myself in such an
undignified manner, and was about to turn back into the
room to find something, anything, with which to cover
my embarrassment.

Before I could do so, however, his face came alight.
He raised a hand to me, not in a wave, but as if to say he

would touch me through the window pane if it were possible. He seemed not to care that the field hand turned to see me in my vernal finery, nor that the lamb bore witness, too.

...

I SHALL JUMP OVER what transpired in the course of that second day at Holland Creek because it oppresses me to think about how much hope I had at that point, hope that Hockaday and I would start building our lives together in the fullness of time. He had been granted a week's extension on his furlough and because I was such a green girl I supposed that would be enough to set our plans in motion, somehow incorporating Baby Charles into the fabric of that idyllic future and setting right the missteps that had complicated our beginning.

Our second night together more closely matched the encounter I had imagined for our first. Gryffth gathered me in his long arms. He studied me approvingly and allowed me to study him. How did you acquire this, I asked, tracing my finger across the diagonal scar that cuts below his beard. A Yankee artillery shell at Chinn Ridge tried to take my head off, he said smiling. I was one of the lucky ones. How can that be lucky? He stopped smiling. He ran his free hand across my mouth, my nose, traced my eyebrows. I should have asked before. Do you have a middle name? I considered fabricating one at that moment. Temperance, I answered ruefully. My mother's wish. His eyes widened and his head tilted at an angle I can only describe as skeptical. Then, for the first time, I heard my husband laugh. His laughter chimed through me: behind my ribs,

along the tops of my legs. Places in my body that I hadn't
known existed rang with the sound of the major's pleasure. Your mother didn't trust to fate, that's clear to see, he
said at last when he could speak. Well "Nancy" is a good
name. And still pretty enough for you. I cannot call you
Placidia—it takes too much time. Shall you be "Nancy"
to your husband then?

I understood that Gryffth was teasing me. I answered
as earnestly as possible that I considered Nancy a better
name for a mule than a bride, and that if he favored nick-
names my family was particular to "Dia," which suited
me quite well. On the other hand, I continued, any name
you devise for me will be agreeable. That's because in the
hearing of it I will think of you and me lying like this,
wrapped together.

He didn't laugh, then. He said nothing, but gazed at me
with unblinking steadiness. In those days his black eyes
were extraordinary, Mildred, for the way they pierced
through all obstructions and reflected whatever they
divined beyond it. Having them focused on you could
be unnerving, as it was in the barn on my first night at
Holland Creek, or it could be stirring in a manner I can
hardly describe, except to say that you understand what
it is like to have a man's heart pressed to yours. I've often
thought Gryffth's gift of sight must have been his chief
asset on the battlefield commanding his brigade for he saw
into and through the landscape with the possessive advantage of elevation that belongs to all raptors—spotting
the rabbit trembling in the log, the sniper tensing on a
distant ridge, and every living pore hair pulse breath in

between—with a perspicacity that was more sense than seeing. He must have comprehended that I lay completely open to him—he had seen how recklessly I conducted myself and how I lacked fear along with strong defenses. As my husband he had the right to take from me whatever he cared to, but I believe in that moment he understood that if I were able to make my offerings freely he would be the beneficiary. Looking at me and into me then, he cupped my chin and kissed me. This was different, Millie. He was not the hardened soldier. He drank kisses from me through that long night like he was dying of thirst and I was the sweet well.

Thinking of that night sustains me, Cousin, despite what followed. The next day before we were fully dressed a servant rode up with a message from the postmaster, telling us that Hockaday was called back to Jackson's Corps. Important campaign ahead, his presence essential, set out immediately. I let myself cry then, just a little. If I had any idea what lay ahead I would have drowned myself in weeping.

By the bye, Mildred: two months after the major rode off on Banjo the fifteen-year-old who put her faith in proclamations was brought out of the woods half-starved. A Frenchman driving fifty souls to the market in Savannah took her off my hands for a few dollars. I regret that now, but I was past pitying anyone by then.

Yours most fondly,
Placidia

248 East Queen Street,

PENDLETON,
SOUTH CAROLINA

August 30, 1865

Dear Cousin,

Did you receive the dress? Was it satisfactory?

I read your letter of August 19 (and by that I signify
that I read your letter *entirely*—modesty seeming to be
one of those qualities rendered obsolete by the upheavals
of the last four years) but I scarcely know what to say. I do
not understand how you and your husband reached such a
state of estrangement considering that the marriage commenced on a note of intense emotional congress. Who was
with you in your household after he departed? What were
the details of your domestic situation?

Agnes Parris would never speculate on such a topic
considering how close she is standing to the target of current gossip, but her supporters (mostly kin and tradesmen
dependent on her custom, as she has few true friends) have
been broadcasting rumors about you that demand counter-
action, Cousin! You will tell yourself that dear Mildred
is well-meaning but lapses too easily into a condition of
being overwrought, a charge I cannot always deny and
work continually to overcome; however, in this instance
I cannot be accused of overstating the need for preemp-
tive action, having been on the receiving end of that lady's
perfidious mischief. I am convinced Agnes originated a
story about me, soon after Arthur's death, that as a widow

I negotiated a better financial arrangement with my in-
laws than I would have enjoyed as the wife of a struggling
attorney, had my spouse managed to graduate law school,
which had been very much in doubt before he enlisted.
How deeply that calumny wounded me, once it reached
my ears! I was tempted to return the favor by broadcasting the rich intelligence I had acquired from an elderly
relation of Agnes that when Miss Oglesby first began attending Miss Murden's Seminary for Young Ladies she
was miserable because she had no friends. Her cold nature
and lack of proficiency in the most rudimentary feminine skills—engaging in good-humored conversation,
expressing sympathy, sustaining loyalties, and the like—
confined her to such solitary status at the school that
Miss Murden suggested to her mother she might be better
off at home.

According to this great-aunt, Mrs. Carlisle, Agnes's
mother Carthene was horrified at the prospect of having Agnes come to live permanently with herself and Mr.
Fincher (and her step-daughter, of course, although I am
certain Mrs. Fincher's concern did not extend to you! . . .).
She solicited the dowagers on the Oglesby side of the family to contribute a hefty stipend, which she paid secretly
to the Cooper family, whose daughter Katherine was also
enrolled at the school (the same Miss Cooper who attended Agnes's wedding, as you wrote me). This retainer,
which endowed Katherine with ample wardrobes in season, music lessons, and the use of a fashionable pony and
cart while in Charleston, required her to play the role of
devoted companion to the lonely Miss Oglesby as long as

Agnes remained unmarried. I can only imagine the relief Miss Cooper must have experienced when she made her final appearance at the wedding in your family's parlor, no less because it was the last time she was forced to endure the attentions of Agnes's libidinous brother, Nolan.

I was sworn to secrecy by Mrs. Carlisle, yet she implied through her tone and by means of a certain sardonic aspect in her countenance that she rather expected me to discount the pledge and broadcast the information. I prayed fervently for guidance on that score, as I might have so effortlessly avenged the harm done to Arthur's memory by whispering a few words into the ears of select ladies in my social circle. It was only with much sober reflection that I convinced myself to keep my counsel, and I am glad I did. I am a Christian, after all, and must not be brought low by one cheek-slapping, but must turn my face in readiness for further abuse, with all the forbearance I can muster! "Do good to them that hate you, and pray for them which despitefully use you, and persecute you . . . Be ye therefore perfect, even as your Father which is in heaven is perfect." (Matthew 5:44, 5:48)

In any case, while Agnes Parris made no mention of the rumors about you and her husband, others in our circle have suggested that Mr. Parris was quite helpful to you in your management of the farm after the major rejoined his regiment and eager to gain intelligence about you whenever your name was broached in social gatherings.

My purpose is not to make judgments of you, dear Cousin, but to plead your case, insofar as I understand it, to those whose good opinions matter. Did you and Floyd

Parris become romantically attached? Were you in one another's company in April or May of 1864 when the child was conceived? If that is the case, I for one would hardly place responsibility for such a catastrophe with you, a seventeen-year-old bride separated from her home and all her loved ones, tutored in the vagaries of matrimony over the course of two short days and left to manage house, stepchild, negroes, crops and livestock with nothing but the sense God gave her and such sympathies as a few neighbors saw fit to bestow on her from time to time. If Mr. Parris is the man at the bottom of this criminal conundrum you must confide this and I will intercede on your behalf. In your communications to date, however, you are omitting more than you are telling me, Placidia. Meanwhile, your precarious position with respect to the judicial apparatus of Holland County concerns me greatly. Please be more forthright in your next letter. (I make this request for your own sake!)

Faithfully, your
(nearly perfect) cousin,
Mildred

Inquest continued at the home of Major and Mrs. Gryffth Hockaday in Holland Creek on July 15, 1865. Mr. Floyd Gilliland Parris age 27 sworn, says he is kin to Mrs. Hockaday through marriage to her stepsister Agnes Oglesby Parris.

I am aware of the charges filed against Mrs. Hockaday by her husband, and while I cannot enlighten the coroner on the paternity of the deceased nor was I privy to the circumstances of this unfortunate babe's death, I may be able to shed light on the severely taxing conditions that affected this lady's mental state in the major's absence. I welcome the opportunity to do so forthrightly, for the purposes of this proceeding.

I live in Laurens for my wife's sake although the farm left to me by my father on two hundred acres near Reidville requires my presence on a regular basis to manage operations. As Coldwater, my farm, lies 5 miles from the Hockaday place, and as Mrs. Hockaday's father Quincey Valois Fincher made the particular request of me that I watch over Miss Placidia once the major returned to Lee's army and assure Mr. Fincher that his daughter was getting on, I made the trip to Holland Creek on more than one occasion to assess the state of the household there, which was in perpetual disarray. Feeling obligated to Mr. Fincher on account of our close connections and upon learning that Mrs. Hockaday for reasons unknown banned the old servant Sukie from her employ, preventing her from tending to Mr. Hockaday's child or performing any other duties, I sent a servant out of my home in Laurens to serve the major's wife. This was a strong, lightsome woman much experienced in the care of children and the proper functioning of domestic life who was instructed to assist Mrs. Hockaday as long as she wanted or needed her.

I additionally assisted Mrs. Hockaday by coming over from Coldwater whenever she sent a messenger to me because of crises at Holland Creek: the first time early in the summer of 1863 because of a fire in the corn crib caused by lightning, which spread to several outbuildings, in which case I brought along half a dozen of my hands to douse it, and the second time because two men posing as government agents impressing livestock and crops but who were in fact poor whites stealing from the less well-defended planters in the area had threatened her with prison if she did not yield her pigs and sweet potatoes. I raised the alarm with Captain Mitchell, as I am sure he recalls, and while we searched the small holding where it was believed they once lived and all along the creek beside we did not apprehend the men.

After that and recalling my pledge to Mr. Fincher my protective instincts were somewhat more aroused and I began to drive over to Holland Creek more often when I was camped out at Coldwater in order to allay my anxieties over Mrs. Hockaday's safety. Her husband had given her his 36-caliber revolver but she had not been tutored in its proper use, so I instructed her. I am aware of the charges Maj. Hockaday has brought against his wife and while no man can fault him for wanting to salvage his own honor from a dishonorable situation he should not be excused from dishonoring blameless gentlemen like myself. Mrs. Hockaday and I became friends in the course of our necessary dealings with each other—she was barely more than a child when she married and the process of maturation was grossly accelerated for her in those difficult months living alone and managing her husband's farm while he was absent on his military campaigns in the north.

Late in the summer of 1863 she received a letter from her husband, only her second missive from Maj. Hockaday in that year, instructing her to meet him in Raleigh, North Carolina, where he had booked rooms for a furlough of several days. On that occasion my brother-in-law Nolan Oglesby was staying with Mrs. Parris and me at Coldwater while the harvesting went on, and the three of us accompanied Placidia to the Spartanburg station where she took the cars to Columbia to catch the Northern line. I can attest that any man with blood in his veins would have considered himself inordinately lucky to have a young spouse brimming with so much ardent anticipation at the prospect of being reunited with him as this lady did. As I understand it, however, while she reached Raleigh in good time and without incident Maj. Hockaday did not show. After waiting for four days without word from him and with her accommodations expired she returned to Spartanburg. Receiving her message I went to town to retrieve her but did so with the unwanted responsibility of knowing how disappointed a passenger I went to collect and expecting that I was likely to dig that depression of spirits even deeper when I conveyed the news that while she was absent her father suffered an apoplectic attack and was not expected to live long. She accompanied me to Coldwater where my driver, Junius, carried her along to Valois. Her father lived one day longer but died without gaining consciousness.

I never learned why Maj. Hockaday did not keep his appointment with his wife in North Carolina and I sensed that Mrs. Hockaday found it too painful to discuss but I believe this was a factor in her declining mental outlook and the ebbing of the natural felicity that those who knew her (including myself) found so refreshing a condition of her company.

After this incident I did encourage my wife, Mrs. Parris, to reach out more actively to Placidia knowing that it was neither proper for me to allay the lady's loneliness nor necessarily productive for me to try as what she wanted, I suspect, if she could not have her husband beside her (and there was never any doubt in my mind that Gryffth Hockaday was the one man who claimed ownership of that affectionate heart), was the shared intimacy of sisters: of secrets exchanged and worries eased. I was not successful in brokering such an alliance. Mrs. Parris is reticent in all situations, but most especially when conducting social interactions, and she has always harbored a sensitivity where her stepsister is concerned. This is partly based on Mrs. Hockaday's natural vivacity and grace as well as the opinion of some members of my sex that Placidia is an uncommonly comely young lady, although I have assured Mrs. Parris that I am not especially susceptible to her charms.

Also, Agnes associates Mrs. Hockaday with an incident involving her brother, Mr. Oglesby, which took place at Valois on the evening of our wedding after we had departed for Laurens. As I heard it from Mr. Fincher, Nolan was drinking to excess and embarrassing the assembly. Maj. Hockaday took matters into his own hands and removed the young man from the party, disciplining him behind the spring house with some benign knocks on the head. Mr. Oglesby was then persuaded to let the major ride him to the small hotel in Traveler's Joy where he was instructed to sleep off the effects of the alcohol and his drubbing before returning to Charleston.

On this count however Mr. Oglesby seemed not to retain half so much ill will as did my wife. Nolan and his fiancée, Miss Willetta Hammond, came to stay with Mrs. Parris and me in the spring of last year. Because of the precarious situation in Charleston many residents of the city had relocated to counties in the upstate by this time, and it was planned that Miss Hammond would stay with us for an extended visit through the summer. Meanwhile Mr. Oglesby meant to set off for his grandparents' property in eastern Tennessee where the proximity of Union forces required the refugeeing of fifty to sixty negroes into southern Alabama and eventually to Texas. Despite the fact that he faced a long and harrowing journey he was quite lively on the occasion of our dinner party and was the soul of civility toward Mrs. Hockaday whom we had persuaded to join us.

In any case Mr. Oglesby was presumed ambushed and killed by enemy pillagers somewhere in the mountains of northern Georgia where his personal belongings were recovered several weeks later and I became embroiled in some serious difficulties of my own with the Richmond government pressing to take 40 percent of my corn crop at almost 50 percent less than market rate, a transaction which would have ruined me. Consequently I was quite taken up with family matters and did not hear from Mrs. Hockaday for several weeks until I arrived at my farm to look over the crops. My servant Cleo turned up unexpectedly telling me that Mrs. Hockaday had discharged her. As I have stated, this young servant was the soul of reliability and possessed a buoyant disposition—she protested warmly to me that she had done nothing wrong, was devoted to her young charge who was growing hearty and strong, and cared as well as she knew how for her mistress's household and her person, but that Mrs. Hockaday had set her on the road that morning with a bundle of food and a gold coin telling her to "make your way to Coldwater and tell your master I will give you a good report but that you cannot stay. I am alone in this Hell and may not keep such decent company as yours."

After that, I did not see Mrs. Hockaday and only received limited communication from her involving questions about the management of her farm for over half a year. We were deluged with rain in January of this year to the extent that flooding killed a significant portion of my livestock. By early February alarms began to be raised that Gen. Sherman's troops, having destroyed Atlanta and conquered Savannah with barely a shot, would not be transported to Virginia by sea as earlier rumored. Instead, we learned that Uncle Billy was planning a campaign of retribution in our state best executed overland, and would soon be on our doorsteps with 60,000 battle-hardened veterans seeking vengeance on the cradle of secessionism.

Judging from reports out of Georgia at the time, South Carolina would be left without a living chicken or a sober negro within their sixty-mile line of march, and every manor house was likely to be burned. I received information of an even more disturbing nature, notably a letter from a friend of G. W. Smith who led the Georgia militia in trying to protect Milledgeville, that at least one white woman living on a farm outside the capitol had been monstrously violated by a pack of Slocum's soldiers. I could not have lived with myself if anything half so abhorrent was inflicted on my sister-in-law through the misfortune of her isolation.

I rode over to Holland Creek when the roads would allow in order to persuade Mrs. Hockaday to evacuate along with Mrs. Parris and me. I was quite shocked by her condition, primarily, and secondly by the state of the farm. She had lost a good deal of weight and was so pale she did not appear to have an ounce of blood in her body. Her clothes hung in rags; neither she nor little Charles were clean. Moreover, the farm was in a dismal way, with many sheep lost to the floods and some outbuildings swept away. One of her field hands had been impressed by raiders some months earlier and another walked away from Spartanburg market the previous summer. The servant who had accompanied her from Valois, Abner, was still at the farm; however he was also much changed in his demeanor, speaking little to me and only asking in a dispirited voice as I was leaving if I would please buy Sadie from Mrs. Hockaday and save the mule from starvation.

At this time I had begun to hear gossip in town about Mrs. Hockaday—that she had carried a child, birthed it at the farm, and killed it there, but I firmly suppressed any talk of infanticide wherever it cropped up, including in my own home in Laurens. I did not ask the lady directly about such things on this visit and she did not confide in me. Instead, she firmly resisted my pleas to evacuate, believing that Sherman would not head west when his advantage, and that of the Union, clearly lay in taking Raleigh. As events have shown, this was his plan, and Holland County was spared. It was my clear impression at the time, however, that had she been mistaken and had hordes of bluecoat bummers descended upon Holland Creek to ravage it and her, it would have made scant difference to Mrs. Hockaday.

If anyone deserves to be prosecuted, and I daresay there are some credible candidates, this inquest should look to the man who abandoned an enamored young wife and a vulnerable son in a war-torn world, failing to provide for them or protect them and denigrating the efforts of those individuals moved to ease their plight with whatever resources they possessed. Her husband may think the worst of her; however, his opinion lacks legitimacy. I do not believe to this day that Placidia Fincher Hockaday murdered her own child and buried it on Holland Creek.

3892 Glenn Springs Road,

GLENN SPRINGS,
SOUTH CAROLINA

September 10, 1865

Dear Millie,

In overcoming your natural reticence, I know you must
have told yourself to "screw your courage to the sticking
place" before writing your letter of August 30, asking me
outright if I am shielding Floyd Parris from culpability
in this matter. In respecting the effort you marshaled, I
will try to answer. My response will no doubt disappoint
you because in this as all else having to do with the last
two years of my life there is no clear-cut truth. My feelings for Mr. Parris cannot be easily articulated. Without
him I honestly believe I may not have survived the first
year that passed in Holland Creek while my husband
was gone, nor could the farm have functioned. However,
he was more than just a factor—Floyd Parris is refined,
cultured, charming, and well-educated (he spent two
years at Princeton before he was called home due to his
brother's passing, requiring him to assume management of
two farms and a cotton mill). In other words, he is excellent company, and that is something I craved in 1863 and
'64 more than I craved air and water. He represented the
world I left behind, and even with his occasional presence
at Holland Creek I sometimes bitterly resented the decision I made that morning in the garden to leave Valois
and part from Father. The part of me that looked to the

past could have been very content with Mr. Parris for a husband, but that was the untested part of me, the Innocent. What I gained by marrying Gryffth Hockaday was a harder version of myself, but a less deluded one. Happiness may not have been a benefit of taking such a man for a husband, but survivability was.

Additionally, as much as I enjoyed Mr. Parris's company and looked forward to his visits, I have always understood that Floyd, while kind and intelligent, is rarely spontaneous in the way people led by their passions are— in the bold way Major Hockaday wed me when he barely knew me, but did so because something in my heart called out to him, as his called to mine. Mr. Parris is calculating in that manner of intelligent men who weigh the risks and estimate the gains before commencing any major venture and who inevitably profit by so much level-headedness.

In March of '64 when he was at Holland Creek helping me oversee the clearing of some new ground on the lower branch I rewarded him with a bottle of muscadine wine I had managed to put up the previous fall. Thus lubricated (and with so little food in the larder that spring this was not difficult to accomplish) he made an astonishing admission. He told me that when he saw me come into the parlor at Valois on the morning of his wedding to my stepsister he was so surprised by my transformation in the two years since he had last laid eyes on me that he could scarcely gather his wits to converse with his prospective mother-in-law. He claimed that he contemplated making some excuse to the assembly and following me back to the kitchen to aid me in cake-baking and commence some serious wooing. However, he argued with himself that I was too young and my father too protective to allow it, in any case. Otherwise he swears he would have made a bid for my hand that very day, his own wedding to Agnes be damned.

I treated this story as mere flummery, and steered us towards less treacherous conversational territory, because I had no delusions about the kind of man Floyd Parris is, and he is not a man ruled by his heart. He married Agnes Oglesby because her deceased father left her properties in Charleston, Georgetown, and Edgefield County which bring in $30,000 per year, and no pretty face could have deterred him from that transaction. That makes me sound both cynical and vain, which I certainly am (or was, at least, when I had something to be vain about). But Floyd's wine-fueled flirtation that night made me remember an incident at the wedding that speaks to this question of choices made: of what motives they reveal in us and of what outcomes they ordain. My feelings had been bruised that morning when my stepmother informed me that Miss Katherine Cooper was standing up beside Agnes as her representative at the ceremony, when I had fully expected, as Agnes's stepsister, to be asked to fill that role. I retreated to the kitchen where Aunt Florie was organizing the wedding lunch; she soon demanded to know why I was sniffling into her potato custard. When I asked her why Agnes didn't want me in the wedding, my father's prim and highly cultivated sister replied, "That girl is as ugly as a mud fence after three days of rain. Why do you *suppose* she doesn't want you standing next to her?"

In telling you this story I understand how relentlessly conceited it makes me sound, and that is precisely the point. Something so minor as a compliment from my normally taciturn aunt altered my estimation of myself slightly that day and may, I realize, have encouraged my headstrong inclinations to reach for more than they might have dared the day before. At the very least, it made me less envious of my stepsister and more receptive to a man, albeit a stranger, whose attentions did not seem to be constrained by the small size of my dowry.

I sent Mr. Parris home that night. I was not seduced by his tales of repressed affections, nor, in Floyd's defense, did he press his suit. I may be ruled by my heart, but that does not make me a fool. Mr. Parris might have been quite willing to know me better that spring, for we did achieve a closeness that I valued and do not apologize to anyone for cultivating, considering how supportive it proved to be. However, I never deluded myself that he was willing to risk his marriage for what he might have had, clandestinely, with me. Floyd knows very well what path he is navigating through life. A dalliance with Placidia Hockaday would never have been more for him than a happy diversion. We did not meet again that spring except in company with others, when I traveled in April to the Parris home in Laurens.

That leaves your curiosity unsatisfied, I realize, when its unselfish purpose is to bear witness against my detractors and serve my own best interests. But I can tell you no more, Cousin. Honesty has become my creed and my salvation; it is my only habitual practice. If by telling the truth I cause harm to someone blameless, someone who acted selflessly in *my* interest, then I cannot say anything. I will be silent on the matter.

Meanwhile, I have a new request to make of you. (With all pride gone, nothing prevents me begging favors from those dearest to me who have already done so much!)

Enclosed, please find a letter from my husband, the first one he wrote me after returning to McGowan's Brigade. I read it so often that it has become soft as cloth. (So few of his letters reached me, and he mine, that even with the challenging logistics of war I believe something was amiss. That something may have been Cowan the post-master, whom I also suspect of withholding a portion of the funds Gryffth sent me. In my initial days at Holland Creek I found this repugnant man too familiar whenever I stopped at the crossroads to mail a letter or beg some salt or coffee from him. One day when I stopped in he struck up a conversation that made me exceedingly uncomfort-able. He used phrases that were peculiar to my husband's correspondence, calling me a "fair girl," for instance. And he brought the conversation, peremptory at best on my part, around to gruesome updates on the war, telling me, for instance, that an attack on Fort Wagner by a regi-ment of Negro soldiers had resulted in the defeat of those recruits by the Charleston Battalion and the 51st North Carolina intent on sending a message: the recruits' bayo-neted bodies had been piled into a mass grave on Morris Island, with the corpse of their commander, a young white colonel from Massachusetts, "being tossed in with his n____s." I was so disgusted by the baseness of this man's expressions that I asked Abner to go to town in my place from that day, and I imposed on Floyd Parris to mail my letters from Laurens. I even took the step of writing to Mr. Hockaday asking him not to send his letters to the Holland Crossroads post office anymore. It doesn't appear that he received that request.)

I fear the major is going to ask me to return his letters before I go to trial, a trial I am coming to accept as inevitable. I won't be able to accommodate him.

If I let him have these letters, it will be as if the pair of us never loved, as if we never even met. He thinks he can obliterate that history because he is attempting the same feat with the four years he spent fighting and serving time in prison for a lost cause, losing one wife in the process and leaving a second one damaged beyond redemption. He has suffered as much as I have, Millie, but he won't accept it. He won't let the suffering have meaning.

So I'm sending the three letters to you at intervals by separate post, guaranteeing that the majority achieve their destination. I've read them so often that I will never be able to get the words out of my head, in any case. Keep them safe.

Affectionately yours and
ever in your debt,
Placidia

P.S. I meant to say that I do not expect you to offer sanctuary to the letters unless you read them, Millie. More honesty, do you see? Griff's description of the war is hard to digest—it will make you sympathetic to him, and I want that. There is nothing he says about me that will make you blush too much, but I do want you to know what was felt and experienced by the two of us if only to give credibility to that strangely intimate separateness that constituted our marriage. Without this evidence to the contrary, I could be accused of having conjured it all.

May 9, 1863

My Fair Girl,

We are at Camp Gregg, Virginia, resting and regrouping after an intense engagement of four days' duration fighting with the 1st SC Regiment and Orr's Rifles at a place called Chancellorsville. In this fight we occupied some of the same ground we were positioned on shortly before Christmas '62 at the battle of Fredericksburg. I hate to think how much Southern blood these stones have fed upon.

We spent the first day working our way through thicket into pine woods where we finally rested with the enemy's breastworks in sight. At daylight Col Hamilton of the 1st brought the regiment over the breastworks and 100 yards beyond, where we engaged the Federals and fought for half an hour or more in open woods, losing good men and eventually falling back to the breastworks. Trimble's division came in to support our lads on the right but the damned idiots did more harm than good by hunkering down behind our line and firing over my boys' heads, killing one of the Company H lieutenants. We began to run out of cartridges and supposed we would soon be shooting pinecones at the enemy but Gen Colston provided ammunition, at least. We fired from our position until we were at last able to fall back to the road, where Col Hamilton delivered the news that Brig Gen McGowan was wounded and also Col Edwards, severely. We held the woods on the third night and slept there in a swamp with roasted bluecoats for company, the pines having caught fire from the battle and cooked the wounded. The next day my lads rushed to get up breastworks with skirmishers protecting them but scouts reported the enemy was moving off. In the night we heard their artillery wagons heading down to the ford.

All together the 13th is poorer by more than 80 men, and news reached us today that Gen Jackson was shot on the 2nd day by some unlucky infantryman out of the 18th North Carolina (thank the stars it was not one of us). He lost his arm and is not expected to live. They say this was a good victory, but Stonewall's wife would likely disagree.

On our first night in camp I was so weary I don't remember lying down before I fell asleep. What I cannot forget is that I dreamt of you, and when I woke before sunup I smelled your skin on my blanket, your scent of honey and mint. From longing for you I was quite useless all day, so it's a good thing we are not fighting the enemy now. I would give everything that I am worth to hold you, dear Placidia. (And now that it comes down to it I can't call you

"Nancy" or "Dia" or "Mehitabel'" or anything but who you are, a name that is music to me, a name that summons you in my heart almost too painfully, like strong music.)

I need to end this letter if it is to go with the courier to Falmouth because I must also write to Beth Wilkerson whose boy Benjamin was killed charging the breastworks on the first day. Grapeshot tore away his legs below the knees—he lived for several hours before he was delivered into oblivion. God knows how Beth is going to cope with Sam gone and now their son, plus her hands running off at every opportunity. I must give her what comfort I can: Ben had the best head on him of any 18-year-old in the brigade and was brave as a bull.

I have had your letter of April 24 and it is good news that you had such plentiful rain—the cabbages will make use of it. I am not sure what you are keeping out when you tell me that Sukie is not "suitable" as a child-minder, but Charlie isn't made of glass and we don't want him growing up spoiled. After all, she took care of the boy when we were getting married and Emelia ran off but you must do as you see fit. Kiss the good boy for me and tell him I will bring him home a Yankee cap box with a musket ball shot through the lid.

Did you talk to Cowan about acquiring another girl to help you at home? Don't let him be insolent—tell him I am holding him to a fair price and he is not to haggle w/ my gullible young wife.

Have you put in the corn? Speak every morning to Bob. He is a better head-man than the overseer was. I

discharged that fellow last year because he tried to pickle
Bob and was soundly whupped for his trouble.

Good night good night my lovely girl

Don't visit me in my dreams tonight or your old husband will go stark raving.

I love you always
Griff

248 East Queen Street,

P E N D L E T O N ,
S O U T H   C A R O L I N A

September 17, 1865

Dear Cousin Dia,

Can they be holding a trial on so little evidence? What are
you charged with? What did Dr. Gordon determine in his
autopsy of the unfortunate infant? (I had assumed it was
not conclusive, or not in any nefarious manner; otherwise
why would he have sheltered you? And been willing to
post your bond?)

I am so dismayed by Major Hockaday's extreme asper-
ity in this matter that I can barely countenance your plea
for understanding of him. With so many of us facing lives
of unutterable loss in the wake of this devastating conflict (*long* lives for the young widows among us), I find it
hard to muster sympathy for a man who would be willing
to throw his wife over for her supposed sins against him
when he has prevailed in the war and she has prevailed
at home and is willing to live together again as a wife to
her husband. On the other hand, since you are unwilling
to tell me how the infant was conceived, my imagination cannot be prevented from straying into all manner of
provocative scenarios, the worst of which make me weep
to contemplate. Such scenarios must be wreaking havoc
on your husband's imagination, God knows, and I cannot help but pity his predicament. What did he say to you
when he materialized at the farm for the first time in all

those months of suffering, his and yours? What did you say to him? How did he look? Was he greatly changed? (And more to the point: what did he say to you on the morning following your stepsister's wedding, to induce you to marry him on such scarce acquaintance? You have never explained, otherwise I could perhaps be less mystified about why you gambled your honor and your life on a man governed by such fearsome rectitude.)

My father-in-law is that sort of man. Having spent so much of his life at sea he has acquired a dark view of Adam's children, believing men to be essentially wicked and welcoming the Tribulation (which he has expected daily for the last thirty years) as the only definite means of cleansing sin from the world. He once told me that Arthur's death was a blessing if only to gather him into Christ's presence before my husband had much to repent for. I was so furious I didn't speak to him for six months; he apologized and made amends when he couldn't bear to be separated from his granddaughter any longer.

Could your husband be influenced by me on your behalf, Placidia, if I spoke from my heart on this matter? Direct me, Cousin. How can I best be of service in unraveling this Gordian knot?

Ever yours,
Mildred

3982 Glenn Springs Road,

GLENN SPRINGS,
SOUTH CAROLINA

September 29, 1865

Dear Millie,

Dr. Gordon knew my father when they were students at South Carolina College. He did not realize whose daughter I was when he performed the examination of my baby's remains; that is how I am assured of his objectivity, a rare attribute in local people of my acquaintance. While the extent of decomposition prevented a conclusive cause of death, the doctor reports that the child did not suffer trauma, and while drowning or suffocation cannot be entirely ruled out, he concludes that he most likely died of exposure. It was not the doctor's opinion that I exposed the baby intentionally—that accusation comes from the magistrate. The doctor asked to speak to me, however, after examining the remains, and that is when we discovered our connection. I learned what an empathetic man he is (also rare). When Dr. Gordon's son was fighting at Second Manassas, his young wife, unbeknownst to her husband, was dying along with her breech infant in Leesville. The doctor was in Richmond on work for the government at the time, or would have been at his daughter-in-law's side. In the aftermath, he worried that his son had developed a very dark outlook, believing there was little purpose in his soldiering when it had cost him the souls dearest to him. Dr. Gordon tells me that he has worked hard to persuade his son that there is a time for war, and when war has been put behind us at last, people will find a way to mend their lives and go back to the full enjoyment of life. That is our natural inclination, he says, and I understand that he means to be encouraging where the major and I are concerned. The soldiers who have lost much will be dissatisfied and angry for a time, he tells me, and may, in their confusion, lash out at the people fondest of them. This will be truest for those who served most loyally, yet for all their courage and purity of purpose found themselves in the ranks of the vanquished, trudging home with little more than the shirts on their backs. It will be more difficult for these warriors, he counsels. They have buried so many comrades, only to find that deliverance will elude them unless they can also bury their shame.

As for my reunion with the major, the moment was unlike anything I expected, despite the fact that I had rehearsed all plausible scenarios a hundred times in the months before he finally returned. Such a gulf stood between us, such a tumult of unexpressed emotions and thoughts, that we were rendered nearly mute by the anomalous quality of our encounter. I do remember that he asked me questions which I tried to answer honestly, if I could do so without implicating others. I took him to the spot beneath the swamp-rose where the child was buried. He wept (I had never seen a man do such), but whether it was for the child, for my sake, or for the wrong done him, I could not determine. One thing was fully evident: he is

not the same man. Nor am I the same woman. Our experiences have marked us. Shaped us. And none of those
experiences are shared. His hand looks strange with the
middle fingers missing; more significantly, Millie, Gryffth
has lost that raptor-sight that characterized his intelligence
so splendidly. His dark eyes are flat—no longer interpret-
ing, discriminating, divining. Maybe he had to sacrifice
that gift in order to survive. Or perhaps it was torn from
him in the violent battery of war. But now he only sees
what is set before him. That is all he wants to see. Or
needs to.

In marveling at how transformed he is, I strive to keep
in mind that I am changed quite as totally as the major. It
is challenging to remember the child who stood up before
Rev. Poteat two years ago with a handful of spring flow-
ers and a joyous heart, who trusted her fate to the good
luck she had been born with and to a man blown into her
path by the prevailing winds. Cousin, you asked me what
transpired when I spoke with Major Hockaday on the
morning of our wedding, after I told my father I would
see my suitor before making a final decision. I shall tell
you, but I doubt it will provide the unifying explanation
your mind seeks.

I knocked before entering Father's study, although it
felt strange when I knew Father was not inside. I heard
Gryffth speak and opened the door to find him standing
at the window Q. V. favored, the Richmond papers lying
untouched upon the desk.

Miss Fincher! he exclaimed, as if he had not expected to
lay eyes on me again.

Major . . . I began, but faltered, not knowing how to proceed.

He was thinner than I remembered from the day before. More careworn. It reminded me that he had lost his wife less than three months earlier and had nearly buried his baby son. In addition, he had been far from home, fighting a war. His face was unshaven and his uniform, I noticed, looked shabby in the morning light, as if he had tumbled it with a bag of rocks before donning it to call upon my father and stepmother. He was as strange to me as a manatee, dear Cousin. Or an Indian chief. And yet I recognized that he was fully at ease with the man who stood gazing at me from across the carpet: he was open, authentic, concealing nothing—not even the diminution of strength and spirits he was feeling, considering his troubles. The scant value he placed on appearances was also evident in the way he looked at me. Since my sixteenth birthday I have been conscious of how certain men, especially those who lack good breeding, study me as if I were a confection being wheeled past on a cart. A gleam of appetite sparks in their eyes as they take in my face; their gaze moves to the rest of me and evaluates the substantive components along with the decorative ones, weighs the whole, and then returns to my face with the eyes now veiled by a scrim of pretense (easily penetrated, if they only knew!) that attempts to feign mild admiration not yet linked to acquisition. The major's black eyes, however, did not rove. They fixed on my face and remained there, as if plumbing a body of clear water for its depths. Because their lucent focus was fully unfiltered, I was able to detect the slightest quality of apprehension fluttering there: not as if he feared to be revealed to me, but as if he doubted his right to engage my commitment on the same spartan terms of self-disclosure.

I cannot explain the impossible sensation that stole over me of knowing this man in the deepest recesses of his spirit, of knowing him as intimately as if I *were* him. Or him *me*. The thought made me blush, but I did not question it, any more than I had questioned the honeybee in my closed fist. Perhaps he read this in the smile I ventured to offer, for he stepped inside the wreath of vines I occupied on the carpet and ducked his head to look into my face.

I am not wealthy, he said at last. Or handsome. And I'm a long way from "refined." In other words, I am not the husband you deserve, Miss Fincher. But this is what I know: to wake up beside the person you cherish and who cherishes you in return . . . there is no better refuge from the world than that. Whatever hardships may come. And they do come. They will.

He took a step closer. My heart was thumping so hard I had to sit down or collapse from lightheadedness. I sat. He hesitated, looking about for a straight chair to pull up beside me, but the only one in the room stood behind Father's desk, and I could see he did not want to take that liberty. After a moment he improvised, resting his hip gingerly on the edge of the desk. His skin, as he leaned close to me, smelled like a sawn plank of cedar.

Despite what I feel, he said quietly—and what I feel is

genuine, resolute—I will not presume to lay claim to such
a tender and unsullied heart as yours, fair girl, unless you
tell me I am correct that in the short time we have been
acquainted, you have experienced affectionate regard for
me . . . ? You "recognize" me, in some way?

He sat waiting for my answer, but not pressing for
it. Because I was too flustered to look him in the face I
studied his left hand where it lay on the edge of the wal-
nut desk. His big knuckles gripped the carved edge, the
brown skin weathered and crosshatched by scars acquired
over the two years he had lived on battlefields and traveled rough country. Without knowing what I was doing
I lifted my own hand and placed it flat beside his on the
desk, spreading my fingers in a vain attempt to increase
the span. His eyes dropped from my face to our hands
and we compared them together: the dark and the pale.
The rough and the soft. The tested and the untested. Husband and wife. We looked at each other then, and smiled.
That's how it was decided. As simply as that.

I believed him, you understand. About marriage being a refuge. I want to believe him still. But lifetimes have
passed since I woke up beside my husband. And I can no
longer claim to be cherished.

I enclose his second letter.

Your loving cousin,
Dia

August 20, 1863

My Dearest Wife,

Did my letter from June ever arrive? And also the one
I wrote at the end of July? The last two letters you sent
caught up with us in Orange County but at that time you
said you'd had no mail from me since the one from Chancellorsville. I won't repeat all that I wrote in July's letter
about the battle we fought in Pennsylvania, at Gettysburg.
No doubt your father will have forwarded you the papers
with this news, as it was a very large battle (or rather a lot
of small battles fought over a great deal of ground). I will
tell you that our division's efforts on the first day (July 1)
played no small part in driving the Federals off Seminary
Ridge where they were dug in shooting Pettigrew's tar-
heels like fish in a barrel. We chased them all the way into
town and took too many prisoners to count. After the
smoke cleared it seemed like the captured ones got off easy.
Our regiment lost at least 100 good men. There were so
many thousands killed before Lee marched us to Hagers-
town that you could have walked on dead bodies all the
way to the Susquehannah.

I was wounded on the third day in a skirmish at the
Bliss farm but it is not so bad—a minie ball broke the stock
of my gun in two and took two fingers on my left hand.
Our brigade surgeon is a capable man or I would not have
healed so well. I told him I have to be able to hold a plow
when I get home and he did his best.

The next day:

While he was mending my hand the doctor let slip that

I am to be promoted. As soon as we were back in camp I
went directly to Col Perrin and requested that he not make
me a lieutenant col. He was surprised and wanted to hear
my reasons. He knows that I know that the governor has a
relation who was forced on the regiment as a captain back
at Fredericksburg when he is not competent to drive the
cook's wagon and worse still he is a little martinet who
punishes the men in his company for the slightest infrac-
tions, like that b_____d Col Coward in the 5th SC who
makes offenders wear signs around their necks, and if this
puffed-up peacock is in line to fill my post I can't allow it.
But I didn't say that. I simply told him that no officer can
maintain discipline in the 13th who has not fought and bled
and gone hungry alongside his soldiers—that poor mo-
rale leads to poor fighting. I also said that my veterans are
brave in battle because they trust field command not to risk
their lives needlessly, and that I could not enjoy my higher
rank if it cost the regiment a single man.

Perrin was not happy but he did not scold me either,
saying there are other candidates for Lt Col who are perhaps less attached to their enlisted men. And when I said
that what would please me more than twenty promotions
would be a chance to see my darling bride he said it is only
fair, considering how the Union army cheated me out of
a honeymoon all those months ago. I will have ten days
furlough, w/ three days to travel each way leaving three
to four days to spend with you in Raleigh (Sept. 16, etc.).
I have already written to Yarborough House in the 300
block of Fayetteville Street and reserved a suite w/ a view
of the capitol, they say. Take two of the gold pieces (out of

the "bank," I mean) and travel light. If Abner can get you to Spartanburg take the Union to Columbia and change cars for Raleigh—it should take one and a half long days or two, unless the engines are all running troops.

I don't like asking you to come so far alone Fair Girl, but if I can't see you this year I think I will just lay down on the road to Richmond and let the artillery wagons roll over me. I have good soldiers in the regiment, brave and generous lads—we cheer one another and don't let anyone pine too much—and many have sweethearts at home they are longing to see. But the ones who are married—those I have not buried with cracker-box lids for tombstones or whose widows I have not shattered with notes beginning, "I dearly regret the news I am about to deliver"—these men understand the manner of living death that an Adam suffers being cut off from his Eve. It bleeds our purpose from us. We can't see forward.

I will leave for Raleigh on the 12th at first light. If you can arrange to be at Yarborough House by the evening of the 15th I will hold you in my arms before the cock crows the next morning. I have so many promises to make to you, Placidia. They must wait until we are wrapped together.

Kiss Charlie
Your loving husband
Gryffth

INQUEST CONTINUED AT THE HOME OF MAJOR AND MRS. GRYFFTH Hockaday in Holland Creek on July 16, 1865. Mrs. Placidia Fincher Hockaday age 19 sworn says, I was married to Major Hockaday on April 9, 1863, at my father's home in Traveler's Joy and traveled with the major to his farm the next day where I have resided ever since. Also living on the farm is Charles Gryffth Hockaday age 3 yrs 7 mos and two negroes: Bob and Winthrop. My husband and I spent one day and two nights on the farm as husband and wife. He was called back to his regiment on April 11 and I did not see him again until the evening of July 1, 1865, over two years later.

On that occasion my husband questioned me closely about the rumors he had heard regarding my pregnancy. I responded truthfully insofar as I was able, divulging the circumstances of the child's birth and leading Major Hockaday to my infant son's grave near the creek. I could not explain the baby's manner of death, not knowing it myself, and I was prevented from relating to him certain details about the child's conception, notably the identity of the man involved, due to a pact forged with my Maker on that occasion and to a solemn promise made to someone who risked his own life to aid me when I would surely have died without assistance. (I am not able to provide this information to the august body conducting this inquest, as sincerely as I wish to fulfill the lawful course of this proceeding.)

In attempting to place this event in perspective for those deliberating, I feel it necessary to recount conditions at Holland Creek during the major's absence with the 13th Regiment followed by his imprisonment in Ohio. During that time I experienced certain difficulties managing the farm, including fires, loss of livestock through predators and natural disaster, loss of field hands (one stolen, one runaway) and thefts by locals, foragers, and deserters. One band of three men who claimed to be from Wheeler's Cavalry but were more likely brigands ransacked the farm in the spring of 1864, emptying the smokehouse, driving off numerous sheep and a mare, shooting a pig, and taking my poultry boy, Davey, very much against his will. They were abusive in manner and threatened me with harm if I did not produce valuables; eventually, three of my hands coming in from the woods caused the men to disperse.

As Mr. Floyd Parris has told this inquest, I did travel to Raleigh in mid-September 1863 at Major Hockaday's request to be reunited with him during a brief furlough; however, he was kept on the march by continuing hostilities with the Union's Army of the Potomac and could not reach me to let me know. It was very disappointing to miss my husband in North Carolina when I had built up such expectations, but even though I did not know the reason for his failure to appear, I understood his responsibilities as a soldier, and it did not diminish the strong quality of feeling I held for him. I am grateful for Mr. Parris's compassionate stewardship of me when I returned to Spartanburg and learned from him that my father was dying in Traveler's Joy. He arranged my conveyance to Valois and managed things at Holland Creek in my absence. Nor was this the only instance when I received valuable advice and assistance from Mr. Parris; however, at no time during my husband's absence did he force his company upon me, pay me insulting attentions, or make himself indispensable to me, as some in Holland Crossroads have suggested. Mr. Parris was solicitous of my comfort and well-being, even to the point of loaning me a servant, Cleo, who was of great help from the time she arrived in the summer of 1863 until I sent her back to the Parrises in July 1864 when it became apparent that I was expecting a child. For reasons that should be obvious I was hoping to defer detection of my condition for as long as possible while I sorted through my limited options. Having another woman in the house would have made that impossible; the male servants, however, did not seem to notice the physical changes I was undergoing.

In the final days of 1864, with the Federals closing in on Savannah, I resolved to keep my negroes from abandoning Holland Creek, as many hands were doing on other farms, by offering the men shares of ¼th the yield. I wrote to my husband soliciting his consent and advice on this matter, believing that he must be in his brigade's winter camp as I had not had a letter from him in many months, however I received no reply. Now I understand that he was in Johnson's Island Prison by this time. Mr. Parris when consulted advised against it as setting a dangerous precedent in the county and warned that other planters would resent me greatly and in this prediction he was proved correct. However I did not believe my stepson Charles and I would survive that winter without radical measures; at the time I was roughly eight months advanced in my condition and my health was not good. With the incentives offered all three male hands remaining agreed to stay through hog butchering that month and into January, when I gave birth to a male baby on Jan 18 with the help of an individual whose identity I prefer not to disclose. The child was alive, but did not thrive during the day and nursed very little.

The weather was excessively rainy that week with some of my fields flooded and the creek very high. At midday on January 19 I heard bellowing from the bull pen located at the bottom of the western pasture. I knew all the hands had gone down to the southern pastures in the rain at my request to drive what cattle and sheep they could find to higher ground, and no one had supposed the water would rise enough to flood the bull pen. I tied the baby to my chest in a shawl and made my way with great difficulty down to the pen to unfasten the one bull remaining and lead him up to the barn. I made it as far as the gate to the first pasture when I saw something floating in the creek. Thinking it might be one of my lambing sheep I climbed down to the creekbed and walked out on a fallen tree partway to retrieve the ewe as she rounded the bend. That is the last thing I remember. I assume that I fainted, as I was still weak from the birth and had lost a substantial amount of blood the day before.

I woke up in the house later that night, wrapped in a quilt by the fire. The child was not with me. I assumed the same person who had carried me back to the house from the creek had put the baby to sleep elsewhere in the house. By next morning when I had not heard my child cry and had not nursed him I became anxious and was told by this individual that the baby had died at the creek and was laid out in the spring house, awaiting burial. At my request this person buried my son in a spot that held positive associations for me; I was too ill to leave my bed but I requested that the baby be wrapped in a piece of my knitting and interred in the sewing box that belonged to the first Mrs. Hockaday as

I could not bear for him to go into the next life unaccompanied by any mementoes of loving attachment in this one. I cannot say any more about the person who saved my life and who buried my child with the greatest measure of solemnity possible under the circumstances, except to attest that this individual did not father the baby and is unable to give testimony to this inquest.

My field hands continued to work the farm with diligence until early June 1865 when word reached me that the war had formally ended. Around that time Abner, a servant who came with me from Valois when I married, took his share in a mule and farming tools and left for a destination in the north with Nerissa, another servant of mine. Bob and Winthrop accepted their shares in parcels of land, my driver Bob at 40 acres and Winthrop at 25 acres on the lower branch of the creek, below the shoals. While the male hands did have differences amongst themselves from time to time and while they did not always agree with my decisions on the farm, at no time was I menaced, insulted, or harmed by the negroes.

CORONER UPCHURCH AND MAGISTRATE Mitchell having concluded this inquest present it with the autopsy report completed on deceased by Dr. Alex Z. Gordon to the Grand Jury of Holland County, South Carolina—1 August 1865.

M. B. Upchurch
J. W. Mitchell

3982 Glenn Springs Road,

GLENN SPRINGS,
SOUTH CAROLINA

October 6, 1865

Dear Cousin Mildred,

The grand jury met a week ago and indicted me. Mr.
Moultrie, the prosecuting attorney for Holland County,
has informed me that the trial date will be set for later this
month.

Mr. Parris has given me a bolt of cloth from his mill
and I am hurrying to stitch it into a dress before that time,
as your fawn delaine has served me wonderfully but its
seams will not be persuaded to hold together any longer.
Does it surprise you that I am able to sew? When the
hands began coming to me with their garments in rags I
understood that no other option was available. I was lucky
to discover a sewing box in the storehouse after Sukie
moved out of it that first summer. (Did I tell you the story
of that woman? I had set off for the crossroads but came
back to fetch my letters. As I approached the kitchen door
I saw her sitting at the table cutting peaches while Baby
Charles pulled himself up on tiptoe to reach the table. Just
as he grasped a scrap of peach and tried to put it in his
mouth, Sukie slapped him hard enough to knock the fruit
out the door. I gathered him up as he began to scream
and told the woman she was no longer needed at Holland
Creek. I don't know where I found the nerve—I told her

I would sign a paper saying she was a freedwoman, but that she had to leave the house immediately and not come back. Until then her manner had been one of perpetual indifference towards me, even enmity, but now she began to weep and beg forgiveness. It wasn't a matter of forgiving, of course, it was the problem of having seen her as she actually was and not being able to get that sight out of my mind. I eventually relented to the degree that I allowed her a stay of temporary duration in the storehouse until she could sort out some solution, but I made it clear that she had no duties in my household and was not to come near the boy. She moved to the storehouse where she lived uneasily for about a week; one morning she vanished with her meager belongings. I did not know until the following year when I went to stay with the Parrises that she had turned up there and Agnes had taken her in. For Charles's sake, I never regretted sending her away, despite what transpired for me as a result of her move to Laurens. That little boy was my boon companion. Some days he was my sole reason for getting out of bed.)

In any case, she left the sewing box behind. It was a pretty thing, painted black and gold, with a mother-of-pearl handle. I took it into the house and lifted the lid to see the previous owner's handiwork embroidered on the underside: "Janet B. Hockaday, 1859. '*A time to rend, and a time to sew*'—Ecclesiastes 3:7." Examining the contents I found a button and a short length of braid that haunted me for their familiarity and for the intimate associations they conjured. I realized that my predecessor had stitched

the uniform my husband wore to marry me. It was a shock
in the moment, but over time my comprehension of the
first Mrs. Hockaday's small and large influences (the uniform was, after all, quite a minor legacy compared to the
child I was raising) was not distressing. In fact, Mildred,
you will roll your eyes and sigh (quite reasonably!) at
my feeblemindedness when I tell you that from the day
I discovered the sewing box I began to feel the first Mrs.
Hockaday's presence around the house and on the farm. It
was not a perpetual visitation, as if she were merely invisible, but an occasional sensation of supportive closeness,
an awareness of being noted. We had loved the same man,
after all. We were mothering the same child. I was never
in control of these manifestations, and they didn't mitigate
the loneliness of my situation to any large degree, but at
key moments during the months while I raised Charlie
and waited for the major to return I experienced a bolster-
ing kind of comfort in this sorority of two. It's as if my
unearthly companion was guiding me towards the fulfill-
ment she had been denied.

Have you had any communication from my husband?
I sent a message to him as soon as the indictment was announced, but there has been no reply. I had the notion that
he might write to you, having cut himself off from the
Parrises, and knowing as he does that I am desperate for
word of my little boy. Charlie must be so confused.

Enclosed is my husband's final letter to me. I read it
one last time before putting it in this envelope. His memories of our sole full day together as man and wife are

essentially as I remember them, except that he said one
additional thing to me under the swamp-rose. He said,
"I wish it were possible to love a woman without hurting
her," as if he already knew it were not.

Bless you, Millie. Do not worry too much.

> *With great affection*
> *and regard,*
> *Dia*

My darling distant girl,

If you are reading this now I love you more than I ever did and I hope you have not forsaken me.

I wrote you in November to tell you why I was prevented from keeping our reunion in Raleigh and to apologize for it despite the fact that I could not countermand my orders or I'd have been shot for a deserter, officer or no. I have seen such things in this war and it is a damned sight uglier than watching a soldier killed in battle, which is ugly enough but there the man's death makes some kind of sense. Two cousins in another brigade, both good fighters and not shirkers, were stood up in an okra patch and shot by orders of the Major General. They tried to light a rag for home when the eldest one's mother wrote that she was being evicted with the younger children. I don't say they were right to run off, but it does strike me as counterproductive to spill the blood of our own soldiers and save our enemies the trouble.

What happened back in September is that orders came straight from Gen Lee through the new division commander, Major Gen Wilcox, just two days before I was to start my journey to you, requiring field officers from other divisions in Hill's corps to come to the assistance of Heth's division which had suffered a great many casualties at Gettysburg. Under Gen Hill our corps marched west to halt Meade's army as they crossed the Rappahannock and we engaged them in and around the towns of Auburn

and Bristoe, Virginia. This was in October. We lost over
a thousand soldiers, twice as many as Meade, and Col
Brockman said the number of our captured might be as
high as 500. Also two brigade commanders were killed.
From Bristoe, Meade dogged us south and drove us all
the way across the Rapidan in November. Harry Hays's
Louisiana brigade and 3 tough tarheel regiments were de-
fending the bridgehead and both brigades took sorrowful
losses, most of them taken prisoner. We tucked our tails
and followed Lee. Not our finest hour.

I did not realize that doubt is a disease but now that it
is eating me alive I understand what happens when questions go unanswered. I don't know if you are angry at me
for Raleigh or if you forgave me long ago and your letters
since then have gone missing. I wouldn't be surprised if
it were the latter, as we saw some grievous fighting this
summer and my men were barely able to move ten miles
before another engagement took up. There won't be a
leaf left on a single tree in Virginia by the time someone
sees fit to end this. We fought at Jericho Mills beside Gen
Thomas's Georgians but the Union cavalry was badly
underestimated in number and there was a terrible rout in
the underbrush. From that day on we've had no camp, just
fighting. Some of the boys are deaf from the artillery—
their gunpowder ruined in the weather—I didn't take my
boots off for two weeks. The worst was Spotsylvania—the
dead and mutilated piled like timber in the mule shoe while
the rain—or blood—poured down for two days straight.
Abner Perrin, who filled McGowan's shoes so ably at
Gettysburg and was promoted to a Brig General, was

killed there, and Col Brockman, the Reidville fellow who commanded the 13th after Edwards died, was shot in the head and lost an arm. His brother Jesse fell on the field but his body couldn't be found.

My darling wife, I didn't think I had a prayer of living through it, and sometimes the fact of doing so is difficult to swallow. I won't try to tell you what I saw and heard except to say that hell no longer holds any terror for me. Sometimes I think I'm dead with all the rest and the Devil's got me dreaming that my life waits for me back in Holland Creek but he knows I'll never see it. Well I must stop such dark thoughts or be borrowing trouble.

Is Charlie still alive?

Are you cutting wheat now?

I sent money to Cowan for you to draw out as you need or spend in provisions. Others from our county have heard from family who are being stolen blind. Pete Kendrick's parents had bacon and a hogshead of salt taken out of the half-cellar. They brought the molasses barrel upstairs to keep it safe, but two weeks later thieves broke into the cellar again, drilled a hole through the floor, and drained all the molasses out. Make sure you are cleaning the revolver like I showed you and bring it upstairs with you at night. These are bad times everywhere but I never thought I would have to worry about my wife and son back in the county. I never figured on that.

I heard the first wood thrush today after the rain lifted. It put me in mind of the morning after our wedding night when we walked the farm and the birds were singing up a riot like they always do after a shower. I showed you

the lambs and the cattle and we talked to the negroes.
We found that spot under the big swamp-rose at the
creek's edge where we could sit and not be seen, do you
remember?

You said may I ask you about your first wife, Janet?

I said I know you are compelled, and you asked me if I
loved her.

I said if I say yes, will that be hard for you to hear?

After a little bit you said No, it makes me glad, if it's so.

I told you she was different, and I loved her differently.
And until then I hadn't given much thought to the way I
loved you, but sitting by the creek w/ your hand in mine it
was so clear.

I said: You are like walking out on a sunny day and being struck by lightning. The force of you. So unexpected.

When I open one of your letters now when I am so
far away and see your handwriting the same power grips
me. That is the only time this old soldier feels *fear* after so
many battles, my fair girl. If there is a hell, it is the prospect of not seeing you again. There is no home for me if I
can't come home to you.

Yours forever
Griff

3982 Glenn Springs Road,

GLENN SPRINGS,
SOUTH CAROLINA

Oct. 12, 1865

Dearest Mildred,

The trial is set for October 26, two weeks from today.

I was at Valois on this day two years ago but it seems like twenty. We had buried Father and I did not know what to do with my grief. I did not understand how one survived day after day, from dawn to dark, waking up in pain and dragging the pain to bed at night. Aunt Florie tried to bury hers by keeping busy. She met with the lawyers and with Carthene and shut herself in Father's study going over his bills and ledgers and promissory notes. She sat me down and told me how bad the crops had been that rainy spring, the wheat and oats, how low the yield had been the year before. She tried to tell me about the debts and Carthene's life estate interest in the house. My stepmother is remaining at Valois as long as she lives and must pay the taxes and other charges, but my aunt cautioned me that the farm would cease to exist unless we could make it profitable again. Florie said we had to sell a good deal of the land and the livestock quickly; that difficult decisions had to be made or all Father's work would go to waste.

I nodded and agreed to everything. I wanted the major so badly. I wanted him to hold me and let me hold him and I couldn't shake the thought that I had done something terrible to cause him not to come to Yarborough House.

Carthene wept and screamed in another part of the house, making a great show of her grief, but she was weeping for herself, not my father. She was weeping for the injury he did her, leaving Valois to me. I couldn't be near her.

On the day arranged for my return, Carthene had gone to town to meet with her own lawyer, to see if there wasn't a loophole in the will that she could fight. Ephraim was loading my things in the carriage and Mercy took me by the hand and led me into the study. She said take whatever you need if it keeps him close to you. I looked around the room but I couldn't truly see it. Without Father there it felt like a stage set. I recognized nothing. Take this, said Mercy, sliding his watch into my skirt. I knew she had set that aside for me at some risk—Carthene would not have overlooked it. Take this and this, she said, handing me his spectacles, his tobacco pouch. I looked at the small table positioned beside his chair. There was a heavy crystal tumbler set atop a book and the tumbler bore a film of whiskey in the bottom. I lifted the glass and smelled it. Remember what he always said when he poured it for someone new, Mercy murmured. *This will have you see-ing double and feeling single*. We smiled together, although it hurt to do so. I picked up the book. Marking the page where he had stopped reading *David Copperfield* was the last letter I sent him, a letter full of lies about how happy I was. It would not have fooled a child, let alone the man who raised me. I will take this book and two or three others that were favored by him, I told Mercy.

When we were halfway to Holland Creek I realized that I should have asked Mercy for some of Father's writing paper. There was none at the farm. And I should have taken some bottles of his sour mash, in case Gryffth came home.

That is why I tried to make wine from the wild grapes that grew so thickly that September. I thought it would please my husband, and thinking of his pleasure lifted my sorrow as I hunted muscadines in the woods. I picked over two bushels and mashed them in a tub in the farmyard. Two of the hands, Felix and Winthrop, were building a box as I worked the grapes, and I asked them what it was for. They told me the racoons would be good eating that season because the creatures had fed all summer on corn and chestnuts and wild grapes, and they were building a trap to catch one.

The box had two compartments, with one end en-closed and a slit cut in the lid to let in a bit of moonlight. The second larger end had an opening for the coon to enter and a smaller hole between the walls dividing the compartments. They showed me how they put a broken spoon-head in the end with the slit. Felix said coons love anything that shines, Miss Dia. He showed me that the coon will stick his arm through the small hole to grab the spoon but he can't pull his hand back through unless he drops it and he won't do that, Winthrop said. He is that greedy. He won't let go to save himself.

I did not share their faith that the trap would work, that any animal would choose death over a shiny piece of coin-silver. But before dawn the next morning I was mix-ing slop for the pigs and Felix came running, calling me to come see the coon. I followed him to the yard and peered through the slit—the box was shuddering in the dust. I saw what might have been an arm emerging from the hole and I know I saw hairless fingers, moving. There was spitting.

Let him go! I shouted at Felix. I knew I was doing wrong to take meat from the man's pot. I told him I would give him half a ham, one of the two remaining in the smokehouse, if he would return the coon to the woods. I turned and walked away as fast as I could and I don't know if he freed the animal, but the box was gone when I crossed the yard an hour later. The sight of that wizened fist wrapped around the spoon's bowl would not leave me, Cousin. Will not.

What have I done, Millie? What have I done? I fear I ruined both our lives when I danced with him in the parlor. Wanting what you can't have is the worst kind of selfishness, I see that, but I can't convince my heart of what my head already knows. (How Southern I am, in that respect: still fighting my war when the battles have been lost.) Will you come? It's strange that I don't dread hanging, but I am frightened of falling to pieces in court when they start talking about my dead child.

Ever so dearly,
Dia

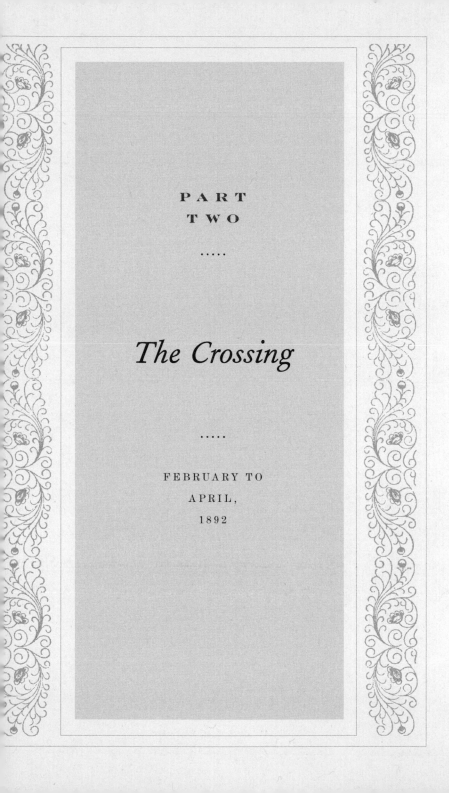

PART
TWO

.....

The Crossing

.....

FEBRUARY TO
APRIL,
1892

February 11, 1892

Dear Aunt Mildred,

I have never felt my shortcomings as a correspondent more keenly than I did this morning while reading your beautifully expressed letter of condolence. It was so eloquent that I caught myself saying "I must read this to Father," before I remembered that he is buried in the churchyard and can hear me no more.

It is hard to think of the Major being permanently stilled. When I was young I considered him omnipotent because his labors seemed to take him everywhere on the farm simultaneously, and I supposed that he—like God—could see into my heart and knew what lurked there. He also had a deep, rough voice that commanded obedience from small children and erring adults. (I was inclined to perceive that timbre differently after Mother once made the startling admission to Charles and me that the first time Father spoke to her she shivered like a tuning fork.)

I know it was initially difficult for Father, as it would have been for Jupiter, to come down off Mt. Olympus after the first heart attack and rest peaceably. The day prior to that event, Helen claims he disappeared shortly before Malvinda served lunch, and as he was never late for well-cooked victuals, she raised the alarm among the tenants, who began searching him out. Winthrop's son found him a mile down the Laurens Branch Road, and when he drew up to him and asked why he was walking so far, my father answered, "I've got to get home. She isn't going to wait forever."

Once recovered sufficiently from that first illness, he was convinced to accede to his quieter circumstances, I believe, because of the pleasure he seemed to derive from marveling at us—his fully grown progeny—who now gathered around him, pledging our devotion—belatedly, perhaps, but sincerely. Charles was the only one kept away, in Europe, where his business concerns have grown along with his family. As you know, Martine is now pregnant with their second child and was anxious to have him stay with her through the delivery.

I returned to Holland Creek from Memphis Presbyterian College and Millie journeyed from Columbia, where she is completing her nursing program. Meanwhile, Helen and Flora nursed Father very capably with help from the neighbor, Mrs. Byars's widowed daughter, who helped bathe and dress him every morning. Helen said he complained at first that he needed to get out to the stables or the racecourse and would put up a fuss until one of them fetched his coat and cane. Once flight was attempted, however, he never managed more than a few steps before becoming so winded that he was forced to rest in one of the chairs on the porch. There he would doze for a time and would then have to be helped back into the house before freezing to death, so eventually he came to accept that his fourteen-hour workdays were done. That's when Helen says he began to allow her to

read to him—newspapers at first, but the news in them
was so discouraging that she cast about for fictional fare
and located the two books I'd sent him at Christmas, still
wrapped in their brown paper in the drawer of his dresser.
Leaves of Grass was quickly ruled out as unsuitable (it
seems misguided in retrospect, but I'd hoped he would appreciate Whitman's egalitarian spirit . . . it never occurred
to me that one of my innocent sisters would be reading the
verses aloud). All was not lost, however. Helen wrote that
Father was quickly caught up in *Huckleberry Finn*, telling
her that he wouldn't mind meeting a man who could write
books just like people talked.

Helen says she sometimes paused in her reading because she felt him looking at her with disconcerting intensity. I held my tongue from stating the obvious—that
Helen resembles our mother so closely in her coloring
and figure (she was luckier than Flora in that respect, who
inherited Welsh goblin blood from the Rhys branch of
the family tree . . .) that anyone entering a room in which
this 17-year-old revenant is standing with her back to you
and that coppery plank of hair falling heavily between her
shoulder blades might mistake her for our mother if they
had known her as a girl, and could be shaken if he or she
had loved that girl too well.

When Mother died of pneumonia ten years ago we were
all deeply grieved and surprised, as she had seemed to be
getting better the day before she passed away, and poor
little Florie made it worse by consistently asking us when
"May-May" would walk through the door from wherever
she'd been unfairly detained. As devastated as we all were,

none of us manifested it as corporeally as did Father. I was shocked at how quickly he aged in the wake of Mother's death. His hair turned from black to gray as fast as leaves turn on a tree. His frame lost at least an inch of stature, and his black eyes seemed to sink inward, losing their shine. We thanked providence for the physical labor that awaited him every day, for without it I think he might have ended that year in bed, or in a bottle.

And yet here's the strangest thing—and I tell you this with the caveat that Millie disputes my theory, saying my imagination runs away with itself and I look for complications and connections where none exist—but I intuited a very particular strain of *relief* in Father's spirit from that day forward, almost as if he had laid to rest not only his life's companion but some burden he had been carrying for her sake. I would be hard-pressed to describe the characteristics of this unburdening, except to say that while he was wildly anguished at the time of her illness, cursing the doctor and hovering over the practical nurse he had hired until the woman threatened to abandon her post, he stabilized once his Placidia left us, cradling a huge sheaf of lilies in his arms as he walked steadily behind her to the churchyard. From that day until his death 10 days ago he was unquestionably sad, at times. Even depressed. But he was notably less turbulent, and I judged his anger to be more slowly ignited than it had been while she was living. Charles noticed it too, before he left for France the first time. He told me, "She has released him."

At the time, I interpreted this recondite pronouncement of my brother's to mean that the Major had long retained

guilt over being captured at Petersburg and kept away
from his wife when she urgently needed him. But I think
he meant more than that, and because I've always been a
bit intimidated by Charles, as clever and ambitious as he
is, I neglected to draw him out.

This brings me to the more specific purpose of my letter, and to the duties I promised to carry out for Father
as his executor in Charles's absence. In one of the last co-
gent conversations we had prior to his death, he asked me
to burn the papers and letters contained in Mother's old
trunk so as to preserve her privacy and his, a territory he
protected fiercely while alive. Most especially, he bade me
burn a certain novel he told me I would find in that trunk
along with several other books, a gold watch, and lesser
mementoes Mother brought back to the farm following
her father's death at Valois in '64. He was most specific
that I should destroy an early edition of Mr. Dickens's
David Copperfield, a volume bound handsomely in brown
calf with marbled boards. With paper as scarce as it was
during the war our mother had apparently resorted to
keeping a diary or journal of sorts by writing on the blank
backs of the illustrations in this book, which number more
than three dozen. With a voice strained by emotion, my
father confided in me that her notes on the pages of this
novel documented certain dreadful experiences he and my
mother endured in the years 1863–65 and bore witness to
his own shameful role in their estrangement at the end of
the war.

We children never discussed this period of our parents'
lives nor can I recall that we ever dared to ask about it,

mainly because we were sensitive to some negative or
even tragic aspects of their earliest years of marriage. We
knew that the two of them had been separated by Father's
military duties, although he never liked to speak particularly about the battles he fought in and categorically
refused to discuss his time as a Union captive. We knew
Mother had struggled to keep the farm running in his
absence, taxing her powers of resourcefulness and occasionally relying on Uncle Floyd, about whom Mother was
generous with her praise and Father tight-lipped. We also
knew that she had managed with the labor of several field
hands, including Bob and Winthrop, who settled on the
lower branch of Holland Creek at the war's conclusion and
whose families farm there still, and others who migrated
north, including the hand for whom I am named, Achilles.
He wrote to Mother years later and enclosed an edition of
the newspaper he was publishing in Philadelphia.

What my parents never spoke of but which I picked up
somehow in pieces was the fact that when Charles was
still quite young Mother gave birth to a child who died. It
seems understandable that they would be reticent on this
episode. Yet there are contradictory elements surrounding
this mystery. As a schoolboy I was often bullied by a brute
named Ned Cowan, the son of the postmaster. Once when
I was eight years old he pinned me against a fencepost in
preparation for a thrashing while I pleaded to know why
he sought so avidly to torment me. Before landing a punch
in my solar plexus he informed me that it was because
"your ma done a n____r." This insult enraged me so
much that I beat back at Master Cowan more effectively

than I have sparred with anyone since, winning my release through the advantage of surprise. I ran home in
great distress, encountering Mother in the garden hoeing
her precious strawberries. She folded me in her arms, asking me what was the matter, and when I repeated Ned's
insult I watched her face turn white as a winter spud. The
fact that I had been named for a negro had subjected me to
considerable teasing from the boys in town, but until that
moment in the strawberry patch I had never considered
the implications of their accusations. I did now, with horror. I complained to my mother that she was wrong not to
have named me Thomas, Edward, or even Gryffth, which
made sense from the standpoint of lineage, anything other
than Achilles. She answered me in a sharp voice I rarely
heard her employ, "You are named for a hero, not a slave.
Go wash your face and stop crying." And that was the end
of my consoling.

I seek your advice on this matter, because I know how
close you were to my mother and how familiar you are
with the history of my parents' involvement with one
another. In contemplating this final request of Father's it
occurs to me that he must not have truly meant for me to
burn Mr. Dickens's book, knowing as he did how much
I honor and treasure books and how entirely they have
influenced me in my choice of profession. (I have had to
concede my mother's uncanny apprehension of how ap-
propriate my moniker would prove to be—no one at the
college considers it ridiculous that a lecturer in Classics is
named Achilles.)

I submit that Father must have been incapable of

destroying the diary himself, so he left it to the next generation (and the one that follows?)—hoping that the power and the pain of Mother's recollections, whatever their subjects, will fade over time and distance, leaving behind only the astonishing record of their struggles, his and Mother's, and the struggles inherent in their time.

In endeavoring to honor his wishes, therefore, I have not read the book—meaning I have not studied the illustration plates, except to note Mother's angular handwriting covering the backs of several in a compacted script extending to the limits of each corner. Neither have I destroyed it. I have been contemplating sending the book to you for safekeeping; I suspect that you were long ago acquainted with the contents and, like Father, have been keeping my mother's secrets out of love and loyalty. If I am wrong in this, I cannot be wrong that you are the best person to be trusted with such weighty memories. If you think it prudent to acquaint me with some general aspects of the story in exchange for this primary source, just enough to be forewarned against any slanders that may reach the ears of my sisters now that my father's role as guardian and gatekeeper has concluded, I would feel that I had discharged my filial obligations as well as my moral ones. If you think I am misguided in my plan, let me know it soon, Aunt. This book burns a hole in my imagination—I have not had a day's ease since Father directed me to it.

Meanwhile, please give my best regards to Roe. I was very glad to see her at the term break last May and to share my city's modest entertainments with her and her

sociable friend Miss Taylor. We have exchanged letters
since that time and I know she decided against accepting
the marriage proposal made by Miss Taylor's brother in
St. Louis, with St. Louis disappointing expectations more
directly than Mr. Taylor, although she declared neither to
be fully suitable. I have been a poor correspondent since
Father's illness crowded out other concerns, even those
I was engaged in fully, and I wish her to know it is from
no lack of interest on my part that she has been met with
silence for the last two months. I plan to catch the train to
Memphis the day after tomorrow and will resume communications with my favorite cousin as soon as possible
thereafter, if she is willing.

Send your response to me at College, dear Auntie—the
address is enclosed. I shall carry *David Copperfield* with
me on the train, bound with a cord to prevent casual pe-
rusal by any stray traveler or train conductor and to remind me of Father's sacred patrimony. Merely by holding
the leather-bound volume in my hands I feel as if I carry
Mother's heart. It is not a conveyance I undertake lightly.

> *I remain your*
> *affectionate boy,*
> *Achilles Fincher Hockaday*

327 Greene Street,

CHERAW,
SOUTH CAROLINA

Feb. 21, 1892

Dear Achilles,

If I possessed the luxury of time, I would make use of it to fashion a complex, subtly persuasive argument in response to your astonishing letter of the 11th, but I was so alarmed by the contents of that document that as soon as I read it I cobbled together this heartfelt plea for good sense which I can only hope and pray will be coherent.

My dear boy, you were not named Achilles for a superficial reason and at this point in time your name must rise to the moment. Look to the classic mythology with which I know you are familiar and review the myth of Pandora. Zeus sent her to mankind as punishment for Prometheus, who made the mistake of elevating man's needs above the gods' order. The box he sent with her, which he had packed with all manner of misfortune and disaster, came with explicit instructions that it was NOT TO BE OPENED, but Pandora's curiosity could not be curbed. She opened the box and out flew all the dark sorrows with which humans have been plagued since time's dawning. Do not let your curiosity manipulate you into decisions you will regret, dear cousin—decisions that will harm you and your brother and sisters more than you can imagine. Not *all* knowledge is instructive!

I say this without having read the book in question—I

only know from the long correspondence I shared with
your mother and from the few times we were able to arrange visits with one another over the years that she did
keep such a diary during the years your father specified.
Since you and your siblings know of your parents' brief
estrangement in 1865, after Gryffth's return to Holland
Creek, I am not betraying a confidence when I tell you
that your mother was anxious to retrieve the book once
she had decamped from the farm and was staying with
a Doctor Gordon and his sister, friends of the family in
Glenn Springs, but had no means to effect its return. I also
know that your father's discovery of the book, made while
sorting through a variety of Placidia's belongings at the
farmhouse in preparation for sending them on, figured in
the eventual transaction of forgiveness requested (your
father) and remitted (your mother), followed by reconciliation. I take no credit for having played a small role in
facilitating this transaction, believing that the Lord acted
through me when He stepped in to engineer this couple's
deliverance from anguished misunderstandings and mutual pain.

What I do not know and cannot understand is why your
mother did not destroy the book years ago, or why your
father did not do so after her death. I would rather not
bear the responsibility of keeping Dia's *David Copperfield*,
knowing what the major's wishes were regarding its
disposition, but if you will not burn it, I agree to be the
reliquary for this artifact of suffering. Only please send
it as soon as you can do so safely, Achilles. Your own
admission that it is "burning a hole" in your imagination

convinces me that you may not be as capable of self-control as I had supposed, and there is too much at stake here to make decisions on a whim. Please wrap it and send it by the next post. I will write to confirm receipt.

As for the matter of you and Roe and her increasing fondness for you, I cannot be happy about this. You and she are second cousins, as you well know, and Roberta is older than you by four years. Mr. Taylor, who is thirty-three to my daughter's twenty-nine, was no casual acquaintance when she and Miss Taylor began their journey to St. Louis last May—he and his sister had visited us here in Cheraw and had introduced us to a number of his friends and extended kin in Chesterfield County, people of refinement who treated us with the kindest solicitude. The man is a banker of considerable stature in St. Louis, and Roberta, had she married him, would have found herself comfortably placed in good society. You cannot expect a mother to rejoice that her child has rejected such an offer. In this, too, I worry that you may be indulging in a romantic distraction without being fully conscious of what (and who) you are risking. Be more circumspect, Achilles, for all our sakes.

Your loving aunt,
Mildred

29 Faculty Hall,

MEMPHIS PRESBYTERIAN COLLEGE,
MEMPHIS, TENNESSEE

February 27, 1892

Dearest Aunt,

The ancient Greeks blamed women for many disastrous conditions, including the Trojan War and winter. Pandora is cast in this mold, but it is interesting to note that she had no say in Zeus' decision to hand her over to Epimetheus like a holiday fruitcake, and even more interesting that Epimetheus was warned by his brother Prometheus never to accept a gift from Zeus, most especially not a dazzling young woman holding a box marked NOT TO BE OPENED.

As with Eve in the Garden of Eden, the later incarnation of this myth, one is likely to view Pandora's transgression based on one's feelings about the offending sex: you will see the moral of the story as woman's careless mischief at work undoing all man's best-laid plans, or woman's insistent pursuit of truth and self-determination in the face of man's (and in both these myths, God's) simplistic underrating of her. My feelings about women in general have been shaped by my mother in particular— and Placidia, while nearly always loving and approachable to her children, nevertheless raised us on a Spartan diet of independent thought, moral integrity, and self-reliance that has shaped our relations with the world, making our paths more difficult but the journeys more meaningful. She taught us that we were never to make a choice based on whether or not it was "acceptable" to others, but only if it engaged us fully—determining what was the course of greatest challenge and what we might expect to achieve if we mastered it. She also taught us that hope was healthy (as you will recall, Hope is the one gift from Zeus that remained in Pandora's box for use by mankind) but that we should never rely on prayer when effort might suffice and we were never to assume that any important outcome "was in God's hands."

I remember her telling Uncle Floyd years ago when he visited us near Christmastime that the only reason the family attended services at Holland Crossroads Presbyterian Church was so we children could benefit from a reassuring sense of community, but that neither she nor the Major "believed." (She did not know that a particular little pitcher was eavesdropping in the hall with a pair of large ears.) She went on to say that Gryffth lost his faith at Spotsylvania, as surely and suddenly as if it had been shot out of him by a Burnside carbine, while she claimed to have buried her God on the banks of Holland Creek. I did not understand the latter part of that statement and still do not but Uncle Floyd must have because he expressed considerable shock before Charles whisked me away.

Did you know this?—Pandora's name translates from the Greek as "the gift of all." I know that is how Mother would have interpreted this myth. If you don't arm yourself with knowledge—if you don't look truth in the face—you won't understand your own life. And in

misunderstanding your own life, you miss the opportunity
of giving it significance.

That is why I believe she did not destroy the diary. Father understood this about her, and despite the fact that
the truth caused him anxiety—even pain—he could not
destroy it, either. All this is by way of saying that I am
not playing at some parlor game, Auntie. I appreciate the
intimate covenant of marriage with its necessary privacies
and pacts, and I am also keenly sensitive to my father's
dying wishes, but I want to make a decision that honors
Mother's life, as well. I may not be able to accomplish that
without preserving the book.

As for my behavior in regards to dear Roe, whom I
know you love fiercely, having been both mother and father to her since she was born, it was not my intention to
interfere in your relationship with her. I apologize. When
she visited in Memphis I was charmed by her wit, her self-
assurance, and her sunny nature and we found ourselves
drawn quite naturally into one another's orbit (with the
disapproval of Miss Taylor, I now see) but I never calcu-
lated to dampen her enthusiasm for Mr. Taylor and again,
I regret very much if I have run that particular buggy into
the ditch. What I can tell you honestly is that I am exceedingly fond of your daughter and through her letters to me
and mine to her we draw closer all the time. If you oppose
me as a suitor for Roberta (and by the bye, she is merely
three years and five months older than me, not four, as
you stated) you must let me know quickly, for the bonds
of affection, once forged, can be difficult to sever.

When I first fetched *David Copperfield* out of Mother's

trunk, as Father obliged me to do, and opened it simply to ascertain that this was the novel in which she had scribbled her notes, a line she wrote jumped into my vision unbidden. It was early in the book, on the back of the drawing titled "My Musical Breakfast," and she reminisced about seeing Father at her stepsister's wedding in 1863. She had known him less than twenty-four hours and yet she says that when she sat in the parlor at Valois listening to her aunt play the piano and looked at the Major standing against the opposite wall listening also, she felt a cord suspended tightly between his body and hers, invisible but tangible, in the way of music, or weather. It was as if they were already connected by virtue of some unspoken pledge their spirits had made to one another. At the time of writing that entry, she claimed that if she stood quietly on the porch at Holland Creek when the livestock were settled and the hands retired, and if she closed her eyes, stilled her thoughts, and let the sound of the creek rise up to her, she could feel that cord running to Gryffth's heart in whatever camp or rough field where he bedded down. Feeling its pull in her breastbone always reassured her that even if she and the Major were to die before the war ended, it meant that their destinies were joined, for better or worse. It meant that finding one another had been no accident.

I tell you this not to alarm you about Roberta but to point out that if she and I become closely connected, dearest Aunt, no one will be strong enough or persuasive enough to part us. Knowing Roe to the extent I do, in fact,

I believe mounted opposition will have the least desirable effect upon her.

...

IN THE INTEREST OF full disclosure, I must tell you that upon my return to Memphis I took away one of the papers in the trunk. It appears to be a legal document of some kind and I wanted professional advice before destroying it. A colleague of mine here at the college is coming over to my rooms tomorrow night to look it over and interpret what he can, although Daniel has already warned me that legal proceedings have changed since it was written and law as it was practiced in the backwoods of South Carolina three decades ago is likely to be a horse of a very different color from what he practices in Tennessee today. This document, dated 24 October 1865 and only partially legible, refers to some manner of agreement being reached between the parties—my father, a man named Walter Moultrie, Esq., and a Judge Abbott—that resulted in the "Order of Dismissal" being accepted by the Court. Mother's name does not appear with the others, but is printed in a passage near the top that is mostly obliterated by a water stain. Was this the cancellation of an annulment proceeding, Aunt?

Always your
dearest cousin,
Achilles

327 Greene Street,

March 6, 1892

Dear Achilles,

By the time you read this letter your attorney-friend will
no doubt have explained the document to you, and you
will have read further in your mother's diary based on that
explanation (because you have too much curiosity and
not enough caution), so I write to you despairing to have
sufficient influence on your actions. Nevertheless, I could
not consider myself a true friend and champion of your
mother's—and of *yours*, my darling boy—if I did not attempt to persuade you once more to have care, Achilles,
and stop where you have begun.

I have known deep love for three people in my life: my
young husband, Mr. Jones, taken from me almost before I
knew him; our daughter, Roberta Delia, born nine months
after our wedding; and my cousin, Placidia Fincher, born
nearly three years after me. My father's much younger
sister, as you know, was Placidia's mother, Geraldine, who
died giving birth to a little boy who died with her. My
own parents were separated—a rare thing in those times.
My mother suffered from nervous episodes that lasted
months and often kept her confined at a sanitorium in
Charleston, while my father served six terms as a senator
to the General Assembly and lived mostly in Columbia.

This meant that I hardly saw him, and when I did he seemed not to understand why I was a tenant in his house.

I envied Dia her loving father and her exceptional freedom, while she envied me my life in Camden, with lectures and concerts and libraries. Before I married Arthur, Dia and I spent our winters together in Camden and our summers at Valois. We were inseparable—and yet we were different. Your mother was growing into an astonishing woman when Gryffth Hockaday discovered her—do you think he was the only one to recognize her for the prodigy she was?—but he had the advantage on his rivals of *speed*. And your father was lucky enough to be the man who claimed her heart when he claimed her hand. She had many womanly virtues, but she stood out from the rest of us (and I'm not speaking about her beauty, which was remarkable but not so rare among women of the best families in South Carolina) for the forceful traits she possessed. In fact, almost anyone would characterize these attributes—the ability to ride hard, to hunt, to debate and to assert herself without masking her intentions under layers of contrived manners, as we girls were all taught to do—as masculine. I suspect that was the result of her growing up motherless, with only her Aunt Florie's extremely liberal hand interceding erratically to guide her towards womanhood. Your mother was extraordinarily frank and truthful in virtually every aspect of her life, and this trait only intensified after marriage. I valued her letters because they were written in a voice of unalloyed probity—of immediacy—as if the words were jumping off the page as I read them. However, I wouldn't have dared to show them to anyone! There were things she revealed to me in those letters—scenes she depicted—that I have never been able to forget. That is why I promise that if you send *David Copperfield* to me I WILL NOT read what she wrote in it. I do not want the weight of those revelations pressing on my spirit when I am reaching an age where I look to be eased from agitation.

After she married and moved to Holland Creek, I heard much less from her and saw her not at all until the latter part of 1865, when Roe and I made the trip from Pendleton to the Crossroads. She had renewed her correspondence with me that summer because she was going through a crisis. As you will no doubt learn (or have already learned) from your investigation, and as I tried to shield you from discovering, a terrible misunderstanding arose in your father's mind—a mind destabilized by four years' exposure to brutal warfare followed by nine months of unimaginable privations in a Union prison—that caused him to initiate legal action against your mother. It was not an annulment he sought, but a reckoning. Your mother did not withhold the truth in order to protect herself, never that, but in order to protect individuals who aided her when no help seemed forthcoming, not even from God. She also did what she did in order to protect her husband, whom she continued to love despite his prosecution of her. The courage with which she faced such travails back then has the power to amaze me still. Your father recognized his error and rediscovered his devotion, thankfully, or you, Millie, Helen, and Flora would not have been born. (Consider that when you hold the yellowed Order of Dismissal in your hands, Cousin. That document canceling the legal proceedings initiated by Major Hockaday is essentially your passport to existence.)

Yet here is where I must repeat my note of warning, Achilles. Placidia's epistles from that time were often difficult to read, as I have told you, for she left nothing unexpressed. I can only imagine how much more straightforward her diary entries must be. This is clearly why your parents did not want you burdened with the information. It is akin to holding fire in your hands, dear boy, and not even the Titan, Prometheus, managed such a feat unscathed!

In loving regard,
Aunt Mildred

Postscript: I was on the point of sealing this envelope when Roberta knocked at my door and requested a serious discussion. My daughter informs me that the two of you have been in near-constant correspondence and that you have achieved a state of understanding about your joined futures that lacks only the word "marriage" to make the agreement more explicit. Is this true, Achilles—that you have already declared your love to my child when you have not taken her mother and protector into the same confidence?

She also astonished me by claiming that I am biased against you because of assumptions made about your income. She sought to enlighten me concerning your financial particulars in a confutation that revealed how intimately she is now acquainted with these details. She told me that you stand to inherit Valois as soon as Mrs. Fincher dies and the woman's life-estate concludes, and that you intend to make the property thrive again with proper management and care. I was too amazed to argue with my misguided child, but I will be more direct with you, Achilles, pointing out that Mrs. Fincher's passing is an eventuality that has exceeded all reasonable projections made since your maternal grandfather died in 1863— nearly thirty years ago!—and that, despite Mrs. Fincher's incessant claims of poor health and poverty, seems no closer to occurring than it did when she first donned her widow's weeds. Mrs. Fincher and, by extension, the numerous rapacious members of the Oglesby clan, are like the wicked tenants in the Parable of the Vineyard—they have plundered Valois of everything that has value while resisting all efforts to make them pay for their ongoing possession of the property. You enter into that den of thieves at your peril—just as the landowner's son did in Mark, Chapter Twelve!

29 Faculty Hall,

MEMPHIS PRESBYTERIAN COLLEGE,
MEMPHIS, TENNESSEE

April 10, 1892

Dear Aunt,

I am reading the book. I cannot do otherwise. Having read Placidia's diary is not the same as wishing to possess it, however. I will send you the pages, torn from the binding. Preserve them, if you will, or burn them as Father intended.

My friend Daniel the attorney researched the legal proceeding in question, taking the liberty of writing to a retired judge in Orangeburg County who he believed might have been on the circuit during that period. This gentleman replied in his letter that he was not assigned to District 8, where Mrs. Hockaday's trial had been set to take place; however, he remembered the case, assuring Daniel that even after charges were dropped against the wife the case was talked about by everyone in the Court of General Sessions for its sensational features. You have always known what those were, Aunt. Now I do, as well.

Roe writes that she has made you aware of her plans to travel here in a few days. I hope you will not make her feel any more conflicted about her affections for me than she already does, but if you do, I am confident that our strong regard for one another will carry the balance against your objections.

Respectfully,
Achilles

Postscript: I am keeping the diary-page written on the back of "My Musical Breakfast," which I believe I mentioned in a previous letter. As short as the entry is, it speaks so tenderly to the person my mother was before she was a mother and when she was barely a wife that I find I cannot part with it. It is my souvenir from a lonely girl whose spirit ruled her life, for good and ill.

Our Pew at Church

IT IS ONE WEEK SINCE MY RETURN TO HOLLAND CREEK FROM Valois. I am keeping busy as Aunt Florie advised and there is no shortage of work on a farm with few workers. Perversely, however, the more menial the task at hand, the more easily my mind severs from my body and flows afar in troublesome streams. Tonight for instance it is pouring rain as I rock Charlie and work sums at the table—the roof leaks in some places but Cleo will not part with her last two pots despite the drips, as she is cooking down peas for tomorrow's meal. With the last of the cotton picked I am hoping to make it see us through spring until the wheat comes in, but Bob says this crop was meager because of all the rain in April. With the blockade on there are few places to sell it in any case. Bob and Felix will try their luck in Laurens tomorrow if the weather clears and the roads are not too deep in mud. I told them we shouldn't need to go begging for buyers when the mill owners are getting rich selling uniforms to the government. I am sending my men to Floyd Parris's office with a persuasive note—I am not too proud to exploit that friendship for my family's benefit.

Cleo has taken the baby off my hands and walked him until he finally fell asleep, but I cannot. My mind is on the major lying in some muddy hut in a distant northern camp. When I force myself to think of something else I see my father lying in the grave, stones pressing on his coffin and tree roots prying at the lid. I cannot think happy thoughts, as my aunt instructs, if sunlight will not rise upon this world.

I am hospitably received
by Mr. Peggotty

A FALSE ALARM SOUNDED YESTERDAY WHEN DAVEY THOUGHT
he saw a man streaking through the woods and two of the hands
went with him to look, wasting an hour of daylight we needed
for burning the rest of the logs to clear the new ground. We are
all still jumpy from the robbers who came in August this year,
pretending to be agents and trying to drive off my pigs before Bob
recognized Junior Mullinax beneath the hat and long beard. When
he told me of this deception by a neighbor I became so angry I
acted without thinking of the danger and grabbed Gryffth's pistol
off the mantel, rushing outside and threatening to put a bullet
in Junior's back as he rode off on my mule unless he stopped in
his tracks. Cowards! I screamed. Stealing food from women and
children while our men are fighting in your places!

Afterwards I had to drink two glasses of muscadine wine to
stop my hands from shaking. Bob asked if I knew how to shoot
that thing and I shouted, Of course, do you think I'd be waving it around if I didn't? I sent Abner with a message to Floyd
Parris and he rode over the next morning with the magistrate.
They didn't find the robbers and they have all cleared out at
the Mullinax place. Floyd set me up in the meadow with a bale
wrapped in a flour sack and practiced me with the Colt until I
could shoot through the medallion on the sack. Before he rode

back to Coldwater I fixed him a plate and we ate on the porch. He asked me why I evicted Sukie from the farm and I told him of her cruelty to Charlie. His eyebrows went up and he said that might explain why Agnes thought so highly of her. I imagine *my* eyebrows went up then, but I didn't respond—I did not want Floyd Parris confiding in me about his wife's shortcomings.

FLOYD SENT HIS MAN George over from Coldwater today with the gift of a young hound—not a hunter, George explains, but a "plantation dog" to raise a fuss when strangers come on the property. I worry about Charlie being bit but Cleo says she will train the child and keep him clear while the hound will sleep under the porch and protect us. I told her I will hold her to that.

Floyd gave me a fair price for my cotton. I hear that women crowd the door of his mill office lately, begging for yarn. I know I should be grateful for his kindnesses but it is hard to reconcile the fact that Floyd Parris paid his overseer's son to go to war in his place. When the hostilities have ceased he will have survived without a scratch on him and will be all the wealthier for it. I cannot determine how that makes me feel.

The friendly Waiter and I

December 17, 1863

Slaughtering the hogs could not wait any longer as we need fresh meat and must fill the smokehouse while the cold weather keeps on. Three days ago the men killed six hogs of good size. I paid Mrs. Byars in hams to help Cleo and me make the sausage, and Bob brought round a freedman and his mother who specialize in boiling and straining the lard and they set up all the jars in the storehouse. There was so much work I fell asleep in my clothes for two nights in a row but it is a good feeling to have a smokehouse filled with fresh pork and to know I have managed one more thing without disaster.

A letter from Mildred arrived today and I was so pleased to have it. She wished me a happy birthday and I saw from the postmark that the letter was mailed from Cheraw in November. She would be shocked if I told her that I had been eighteen years old for two days before realizing it—my birthday had come and gone and I was too busy to pay attention. I don't know if that is a good thing or a bad thing. It is probably good.

Davey, the boy who takes care of the poultry (and who may have been Sukie's grandson—I'm not certain—but who has never expressed the slightest displeasure at her expulsion) has a talent for entertaining children. Charlie crows with delight whenever the young man comes on to the porch with the morning's eggs, and Davey takes him on his shoulders and bounces him around the yard while crooning some wordless tune that pleases the boy beyond any lullaby I have ever sung off-key. He is the one who informed me that Charlie's birthday is the 22nd, the day of the solstice, or I should not have known the little man will be two years old by Christmas.

Steerforth and Mr. Mell

I SUPPOSED IT WOULD BE A VERY LONELY CHRISTMAS BUT Aunt Florie surprised me, riding over in her carriage from Glenn Springs where she is staying with an old school friend and her family. She has already moved out of Valois and is readying a small house in Summerville. I sometimes forget how wealthy my aunt is in her own right as she is so much nicer and more intelligent than any wealthy people with which I have had acquaintance (the Oglesbys, for instance).

She brought Charlie a painted horse to pull, and for me it was as if she had consulted with the angels who told her what I prayed for daily. A keg of salt, three skeins of wool yarn and several spools of cotton thread, three pounds of coffee and a quart jar of raspberry jam, women's leather boots to replace the oversized pair of Gryffth's I have worn to shreds, and a bottle of Father's sour mash ("for your dispensary, of course"). Also a beautiful quilt of sea-green silk, which she insists is warmer than it looks and therefore practical despite appearances to the contrary.

Cleo and I managed to cook a respectable meal and I surprised myself being so puffed up over the turkey, which was one of twelve we raised from chicks and was quite the best fowl I've ever eaten. There was fried sausage, turnips, and a nice custard, which we spooned up with the jam.

After supper Aunt sat me down with the yarn and taught me how to knit—she is writing out a simple pattern so I can make a warm vest for Charlie. When we had made good progress we helped ourselves to one glass each from the dispensary. She asked me what news from my husband—she knew about my disappointing trip to Raleigh—and I told her there had been no more letters since the one instructing me to go there in September. Aunt Florie never voiced opposition to my marriage, but now she worries that I am being wasted here at Holland Creek. She says that I am too smart for my own good and too soft-hearted, when what's needed here is an overseer rather than a wife. I tell her we are building a home for our future family, the major and I—that the farm is central to everything that follows, and because of that no one will safeguard it as I will. I hope I am right. At least let me help with the farming part of that, my aunt says. You don't have enough hands for the work that needs doing. Some look on my face must have caused her to add quickly: your husband may settle up with me when he returns. Meanwhile, who in Holland Crossroads should I speak to about hiring servants? I told her Cowan the postmaster seems to be the only one in that line but that he is not a savory figure. Aunt Florie assured me she is not intimidated by men of that kind, having been required to manage Valois through the years as best she could, given Father's disinclination for business and for businessmen.

The next day Aunt Florie took her buggy into town, telling me I need not trouble myself about the business and that she would pay all costs. I don't know what arrangement she reached with Cowan but I have no doubt he cheated her. The two men he brought to the farm the next day, Cato and Isaac, are strong-looking, but something about them troubles me, each in his own way. Isaac wouldn't look directly at my aunt when she spoke to him—nor me—and still won't. He wipes spittle from his mouth repeatedly as if something prevents him from swallowing. Cato is a big man, perhaps as much as two hundred pounds, with hands the size of shovels. As big as he is, he has a hungry look about his face that makes me think his name should be Cassius, not Cato, from Caesar's line to Marc Antony: "Yond Cassius has a lean and hungry look; he thinks too much: such men are dangerous."

I didn't foresee that Bob would be so put out by Aunt Florie's charity—he has been kicking sand ever since the new hands set foot on the farm, not pleased, as I had expected. I see that it was wrong not to prepare him, at least.

Changes at Home

An ICE STORM HAS BROKEN TREES IN THE ORCHARD AND suspended activity outdoors for three days. Charlie became ill on the storm's first day and we sat up with him until his fever broke. On the second night it grew so cold in the upstairs room where he sleeps with Cleo that when she lifted him out of his cot the next morning his wet diaper steamed. I succumbed to the same sickness and for several days Cleo has been nursing us both downstairs by the fire.

I asked Cleo to send Bob to me this evening for a report and she made a face. When he came up to the house I understood why—he was angry about the new hands and is glad of an audience to declaim them to, tirelessly.

With the sun out today and the air milder, he had the men taking down the large water oak in the cow pen that was split by the weight of the ice. He says Isaac is playing at being sick and the big one, Cato, argues with Bob about every instruction and tries to pick fights with the others but they are too frightened of him to get drawn in.

I ain't afraid, Bob said to me, I'll wear him out with the cowhide if he gives me cause.

I dread such an encounter between the two—I don't give Bob good odds if Cato decides to push the conflict. I told Bob to send one of the hands with Isaac to Dr. Jolley in the morning and fetch some medicine, hoping this will defuse the tension incrementally. If Bob cannot handle the new man, however, I will not have many options.

There is always the Armory, I tell myself, and it chills me to realize what a short time was required to turn me into one of those people who cannot afford the luxury of mercy. The second more chilling realization is that this is what Cowan may have planned for me. He thinks I am cut from the same cloth as the Charleston types who are too refined to know how a pig makes its way to their plates—who have never worked alongside their servants and who make it someone else's business to correct them.

I have never minded work. But when it comes to forcing others to work, I dread the prospect of proving myself to be incompetent in this capacity almost as much as I fear the possibility of excelling at it.

Mrs. Gummidge casts a damp on our departure

I AM WELL ENOUGH TO SIT BY THE FIRE AND DO SOME MENDING today, although my eyes are sore and do not take well to needlework—they feel as if they have been rolled in nettles. Charlie seems a little better—Cleo put a plaster on his chest last night and this morning he is coughing less and wants to eat.

Before supper, Winthrop returned from town alone. He brought the bad news from Dr. Jolley that Isaac is afflicted with an abscess on his molar that has gone untreated—it has infected the jaw so badly it is gangrenous. Jolley offers to make the man comfortable at his infirmary as he is past treatment. I say a prayer for Isaac while cursing myself for my gullibility. Now I am feeling even more fatalistic about Cato.

My magnificent order
at the public-house

January 21, 1864

THERE HAVE BEEN SOME DREADFUL DRAMAS UNFOLDING OVER the past several days at Holland Creek, but viewed through the superior lens of hindsight it is clear that progress could not have been made without these struggles. Isaac died at Dr. Jolley's on Tuesday. I do not know where he came from nor how far-flung his kin may be, but it does seem a sorry thing to die alone among strangers through no fault of your own but the fault of misfortune. This news seemed to unsettle the hands, who had little time to know the man and no experience of him as a healthy soul but still experienced his death as a foreshadowing of their own mortalities. Cato's response was to redouble his efforts at fomenting chaos, insuring that the other men carry on in constant fear of his giant fists.

I was determined to get the Irish potatoes planted this week and to move some young trees in the orchard to replace those lost to ice, but lacking hands for the work needing to be done, I directed Bob to hire a man for the two or three days it would take. He hired Ransom from the Byars, who came on Thursday with his ten-year-old son, Prince. Ransom is known for his green thumb—Bob says if the man drops a nut in his pocket in the morning, by nightfall the nut will have sprouted. This gift for propagation is said to be passed down to Prince so I was glad for their work on the trees and potatoes, but something went amiss the second day. In digging up the seedlings Ransom cautioned Cato not to tear on the rootballs like pulling legs from a turkey or the trees would yield poorly and Cato answered that he would not be bossed about by a poxed-over worm. (Ransom survived smallpox as a child and bears the scars on his face and his scalp.) The disagreement escalated from there but none of the men who were present in the orchard will tell me exactly how it did nor what was said. What Bob, Winthrop, and Felix can agree on is that Cato clapped a spade down on Prince's head when he tried to defend his father, causing the boy to be briefly unconscious, although he seems to have recovered. This is how I related the story to Mr. Byars when I drove Ransom and his son back to his farm, the boy lying in the wagon bed with a compress of cold creek water on his head and two dozen of Cleo's best sausages tied in a sack as consolation for Byars. He took the news and the sausages in good humor but I was not feeling so sanguine. I drove straight from there to the post office and stood up to Mr. Cowan in a voice I did not know I possessed, telling him he was to come directly to the farm to take Cato away and he should bring a full refund of my Aunt Fincher's fee—that if I could not use it to buy labor, I would buy some peace with it, at least.

*I make myself known
to my Aunt*

COWAN WAS NOT PLEASED, BUT NOW THAT HE KNEW MR. BYARS
had been acquainted with the story of the murderous servant-
for-hire, and knowing that soon all the other farmers on the
crossroads would have heard the cautionary tale, he had little
choice but to undo some of his mischief. He arrived yesterday
morning with two unsavory-looking assistants bearing bullwhips
and chains. They bound Cato following a protracted struggle in
the cowshed, which was audible to all if mercifully not visible.

As the two goons pulled Cato from the shed and sweated
through the process of subduing him long enough to chain his
manacles to the back of Cowan's buckboard, the negro spied me
watching from the porch and twisted his frame in the effort to
pull his right arm free above their heads. Everyone saw it—me,
Cowan, Abner on the step below, the other servants watching
open-mouthed from the relative safety of the carriage shed. Even
the dog on her chain, who had been barking at Cowan's men, set
up a frenzied howl when Cato fixed his gaze on me.

His teeth were gritted and his body rigid, shaking slightly,
as if it took all his formidable strength to lift his limb into position, pointing a finger straight at me. He did not say a word as
he stood there. But he pointed. Cowan drew the bullwhip back
and brought it down on Cato's shoulders.

A sleety rain was starting to fall as the strange procession moved out of the farmyard. My hands and feet had gone numb but I kept watching from the porch to make certain the crew was well shed of my property. I was remembering the look on Gryffth's face when we rode away from the post office on our wedding day, leaving the Wilkersons' pair of runaways in Cowan's charge. It was an expression that forecast heavy weather: a storm on its way that could not be averted. I wondered now if my face wore that expression, for I was feeling sick dread from my head to my frozen feet, thinking that when the storm came there would be nowhere to shelter.

We have missed our chance of potato-planting, for now.

The momentous interview

Today dawned clear and cold. I sent Abner to the Hambrights four miles down the road with one of my smaller cows as we have only enough oats for the two better milkers. Edna Hambright is going to weave up some of my wool in exchange, at least fifty pounds. The men have cleaned out the icehouse and will be hauling ice from one of the neighbor's ponds today. I was preparing to go into town to sell four crocks of my best lard, choose seed for the garden, and get a piece of harness repaired. I wrapped my shawl around me and was tying on my bonnet when Abner rapped at the laundry room door.

Why aren't you halfway to the Hambrights? I asked, vexed. His expression was a strange one—I couldn't tell if he was frightened or excited. There is someone come to the farm who wants to see you, Miss P. He's in the barn.

He was trying my patience and I had little to spare that day. If he requires my presence then he had best knock on my door, I told Abner. But he should do it some other day, for no one will answer if he knocks now. I was already making my way to the carriage shed, where Abner had harnessed the pony to the small wagon. Please Miss!, he called after me. He daren't come out.

I turned to look at Abner to see if what I heard in his voice was also written on his face. It was. He was upset.

I set my satchel in the wagon and took a deep breath (I was growing accustomed to expecting calamity around every corner) before following Abner into the barn.

It's Missus Hockaday, he called out to the draft horse and two red chickens strutting in the straw. No one else was there. I listened to the silence, feeling ridiculous. Abner, I began—but a noise from deep in the barn's interior silenced me. I watched the lid of a hogshead slide off and a shadow unfold itself from the barrel. I stepped backwards towards the door, trying to determine what I was seeing.

Come into the light, I said.

When the shadow moved into the light cast by the hay mow I saw a figure covered in dark syrup. The syrup made no sense to me. I sought out the figure's face and looked into one blazing blue eye. If he had a second eye, it was swollen shut, or covered in syrup. At last, I understood. The syrup was blood. The shadow-man was covered so thickly in blood that there was blood congealing in his shoes.

Have you killed someone? I cried.

The man made a noise. He shifted. His bloody lips parted. No, ma'am.

I remembered the figure, of course. He was the servant in the woods I had encountered on my wedding day: the blue-eyed negro who ran away from the Wilkersons' farm with his snake-bit companion.

That is all your blood?

Yes, ma'am.

I looked to Abner, who watched from his corner, frightened. Who has drawn it? Has Cowan done this to you?

No, ma'am. The missus hired an overseer.

Mrs. Wilkerson hired a man?

Yes, ma'am.

Why did the overseer whip you so badly?

On account of the pinewood, ma'am. Cutting in the pinewood.

Even with only one blue eye staring back into mine, I felt a recurrence of the affinity I had experienced in the pignut clearing, some quality in this young man that spoke to me from across our formidable social divide, and now, across vast territories of experience we could not share. Whatever violence had visited him, it did not warn me off, as it should have.

I asked, Aren't you serving in the house?

No, ma'am. Not since Master Sam got killed at Ox Hill.

I nodded, remembering what Gryffth had written to me about Sam Wilkerson being killed in '62 and his son Ben dying in Gryffth's own regiment at Chancellorsville last May. All right, I said.

You were cutting in the pinewood.

I return to the Doctor's
after the party

HE SAID, IT WAS WARMER YESTERDAY AND CASH THE OVER-seer was sure the sap was rising. The missus fixes to sell fifty cords of stove wood and everyone knows the wood don't burn best once sap rises in the pinewood.

So he had all hands in the wood.

Yes, ma'am. And Mose is lame. He carpenters and he can build most anything but Cash say he don't care if he the Second Coming—Cash put him in the pinewood and Mose couldn't keep up. Cash whip him to put more muscle to the axe and it only lays him out. I'm beholden to Mose on account of the snakebite that made him crank-sided so I tell Cash I'll do for Mose and Cash say you'll do for six men if I tell you to and Mose can chop his share of wood or go to hell. When he go to whip Mose again I grabs the cowhide and says if there's any lick struck I will strike the next. He fetches the driver and they drags me to the barn. Cash lays on forty hard and pours salt brine over that.

They pickled you?

Yes, ma'am. And forty more. Then salt and red pepper a second time. Then Cash cuts me down and says here's the good news: next time you interfere on me you'll be dead before you reach the barn.

Abner spoke up. He can't go back, Miss P. Cash already beat a girl so bad he knocked her eyeball out.

I turned back to the bloody man.

What's your name? I can't call you Blue Eyes.

He made a sound. It was like someone exhaling after holding his breath a long time. It's Titus, ma'am. But if you call me that name, Cash will find me for sure.

And if I don't turn you over right away, there will be hell to pay. I can't afford to compensate Beth Wilkerson, either.

No, ma'am. But I know you short-handed. I work sunup to long after sundown, if need be. I'm wicked good with a plow, good with horses and cattle. I mend fences, shear sheep, know my way around cotton—

You'd better be, I interrupted. Because Bob is a fearsome taskmaster.

He said, I know that, ma'am. Mose tell me.

I waited to hear more.

Mose say Mister Cash the bossman Major Hockaday sacked. Missus Wilkerson got him cheap. Cash the one Bob whupped.

I studied this young man more carefully, feeling that I had already been outmaneuvered. He used the back of his hand to wipe sweat and dried blood away from his swollen eye, revealing a sliver of blue to match the undamaged eye.

Were you raised up on Wilkerson's, I asked.

No, ma'am. I was born on a big place in a far county. Ma carried me off when I was little.

Where's your ma now?

Dead a long time, missus.

Any other family?

My mother's brother. In Sumter. If he still alive.

Somebody turns up

I THOUGHT CAREFULLY ABOUT MY DECISION. WITH SPRING coming we would be woefully short-handed, especially if we lost Abner, whom my stepmother had been pestering me to return. Blue Eyes might make a good field hand if he recovered from his beating, and without family ties in the area there was less risk from gossip getting out about his identity. It was not right that I should profit from Beth Wilkerson's loss—a war widow struggling to hold on to the farm for the sake of her remaining children. However, my father taught me that only foolish or sadistic planters caused lasting injury to their servants. If Mrs. Wilkerson employed an overseer on his way down, a man who had proven himself a brute at Holland Creek and who treated her own hands barbarically, she could not be a wise woman. The thought occurred to me that she may benefit from the lesson of losing mistreated servants if it served to make her more invested in her family's interests. Besides, there was something in this pitiful young man that clamored for my care.

I will allow you to stay through the night, I told him. Perhaps two nights. After that I will have to write to Mrs. Wilkerson. It is my duty.

He nodded. I'm obliged.

How will you keep the others from turning you in? There will be a reward.

Abner shook his head. They won't tell. Bob and Winthrop.

Felix. They hate Cash. They know what he will do to this one if he's sent back.

The two men watched me silently while I considered the situation.

What am I to call you then, I asked the runaway. It can't be Blue Eyes.

He thought. My uncle was a good man. Strong. I'll take his name, ma'am. Achilles.

I agreed. You can wash in the horse trough, I said. Burn those bloody rags—Abner will bring some clothes. Sleep in the hay mow for now and you can work tomorrow. But lay low, the patrollers will be searching here eventually.

All the way to the crossroads I thought to myself: I am a criminal now. I must write to Beth Wilkerson as soon as I return to the house, or there will be no redeeming me. But when I drove the wagon home in the afternoon and sat at Gryffth's desk there was no paper in the drawer. I had forgotten to buy it while I was in town.

My first fall in life

SNOW ON THE GROUND, MELTING BY NOON. THE FIRST LAMB born today. I wanted to bring her in the small pen for the night, but Felix says no matter how often they patch the fence between that pen and the hog pen, the sows find a way to get through and eat the lambs. Bob agrees: he says we must let the lambs born this week take their chances with the flock despite the cold. How comfortless the world!

I had a letter from Aunt Florie in Summerville, where a letter from the major caught up with her after going first to Valois. He has written to her asking if she has news of me—if I am well— and telling her he has not heard from me since his furlough was cancelled and is worried I do not think of him. Not think of him! The other half of my heart. I only wish she had enclosed his letter so I could hold his writing in my hands and feel the wholeness of him again. Sometimes I think I no longer recognize what is real and what I have fabricated in my mind to make the real parts more palatable. I wrote to him before Christmas and sent the letter by way of the Parrisses, as I cannot trust Cowan, but I must ask Floyd if it was mailed.

The injustice of the situation is so grating that I cannot allow myself to think much about it: that while my husband is fighting for ground at the northern limits of the war and unable to obtain leave, back here in home-country we are beset by every manner of shirker, deserter, renegade, bandit, and bummer. The worst are the Confederate agents, who arrive unannounced at backcountry farms in order to catch out the best livestock and stores and carry them off under authority of their trumped-up "impressment" law. This is nothing but a license to steal from those of us who have already given our greatest treasures—our fathers and brothers and husbands. The richest families—those fire-eaters who yelled the loudest for secession—have incurred little cost, from where I sit.

There are times I wish we would lose this conflict soundly, if only to have a full accounting of what has been lost and then move on. I know I am too proud. But I believe I could survive in a new world, if it comes, considering what I have learned this past year and how I have worked. And yet there are people I once knew well, people I once called kin, who look down on me for this acquired pragmatism. I am no longer their social equal. Thank the Lord for that.

ACHILLES, THE RUNAWAY, HAS been working since his second day here. His face has nearly healed, although it will be scarred, and he favors his right arm, as the butt of the bullwhip cut a gash in the left. I offered to send him to Dr. Jolley but he was fearful of detection. Cleo made him a dressing for the arm and says it is on the mend.

The other hands seem well disposed to him—even Bob, surprisingly—and I am grateful for his capability and calm disposition after the twin disasters of Isaac and Cato. After the sun came out and the snow melted, Achilles harnessed Sadie and commenced throwing down the corn beds where we are to plant oats. I watched him from the cow pen where I'd gone to check progress on the tree, and the slope of his broad back resonated for me in a strangely comforting way. Even more strangely, while I watched the young man plow, I sensed the first Mrs. Hockaday standing behind me, watching too. I have accepted her presence as reassurance that my law-breaking is justified. It's unlikely that my husband would approve, but Gryffth is not here. I am going to let him stay.

We arrive unexpectedly at
Mr. Peggotty's fireside

I HAVE WORKED OUT A DRILL THAT BOB IS UNDER ORDERS TO practice with the men—an essential protocol for hiding hams, sacks of potatoes, flour barrels, jars of preserves, molasses, and salt; for driving geese out of the yard and down to the pond and for scattering the pigs and sheep in the woods. Achilles knows to lead Sadie and the two cows upstream on the deer path to the hay meadow and to stay hidden while they graze. We have used this routine twice now, once when there was a false alarm and once successfully when patrollers came through looking for Achilles and a young female servant who fled with her baby from the Andersons down the road. I was able to fob them off with two geese and a few sacks of middlings, telling them we had no runaways but appreciated their vigilance.

This morning just as the sun cleared the ridge, Gopher woke me with her barking. Three men rode into my yard and began snatching up hens before I'd even stepped out on the porch with Gryffth's revolver in hand. The man who appeared to be in charge was a sour-looking brute with guns bristling from his belt and so many lumps on his face and forehead that he might have been a gourd. He barely gave me a nod, calling out that he was Lieu-tenant Williams in Wheeler's Cavalry and these horsemen were a contingent who had fought with Longstreet in the Knoxville campaign. They needed supplies for the brigade and Tennessee was tapped out.

I said I can't say I'm surprised if this is how the army keeps itself fed, but whoever you are you won't strip us clean while I have lead in this firearm. He laughed at that and looked around the yard, where no servants showed themselves. Abner, Achilles, and Davey must have been alerted and had followed my instructions to drive the stock out of sight, while Bob, Winthrop, and Felix were already down in the fields.

Williams swung off his horse, kicking Gopher, who dove under the porch. He took the steps in two strides and snatched the Colt out of my hands, tossing it to the red-bearded man who held one of my hens by the neck. I will follow you to the smokehouse, he said, smiling, showing big teeth stained yellow by tobacco.

There was nothing for it. I walked to the smokehouse taking as much time as I dared, but none of my servants appeared. I made a show of trying all the keys, but he stood so close behind me that I was too uncomfortable to remain pushed up against the door, and swung it open. The cavalryman sighed with satisfaction. On the spikes lining the walls and hanging from the scantlings timbers were hams and shoulders, planks of bacon and sausages. Winthrop had kept a good fire smoldering in the center of the room, and the aroma of smoked pork rolled over us as the heat rushed out the open door. I sought the man's face with my eyes. I have a child, I said. A little boy. My husband is an officer in General Hill's Corps and has fought bravely at Gaines' Mill, Frayser's Farm, Second Manassas, Ox Hill, Fredericksburg, Chancellorsville, and Gettysburg. If you are a true soldier and a gentleman you will not leave his family to starve.

The man studied me for a moment, no longer smiling, before calling over his shoulder: Linder! Hite! Over here!

They all descended on the meat, using sacks to carry off as much as they could. I retreated from the smokehouse and hurried to the henhouse—under one of the nesting boxes I had hidden the Scottish sterling tea set Father gave us as a wedding gift. The chickens made a commotion despite my shushing and it shouldn't have surprised me that the egg door opened and Davey peeked in. Take this, I whispered, pushing the teapot through the opening. Drop it in the shallow part of the creek, where we bathed Charlie last summer. Davey's hands were shaking, but he took the pot and a filigreed cream jug and as I was stuffing straw back in the box and snatching up a hen to settle my hands the door behind me opened and the man with yellow teeth was there, his gun drawn. He took me by the wrist and pulled me outside where Davey stood, ashen, a horseman's revolver at his back. My captor nodded at the third bandit and the man bagged the teapot and the jug.

Now let's tour the house, missy. He pushed me across the yard and through the doorway. Gold, silver, jewelry, whiskey, firearms. Don't waste time, he told me.

I make the acquaintance
of Miss Mowcher

I worked as speedily as I was able, not wanting to be alone with him in case he remembered some other commodity I could provide, and realizing for the first time that morning that I was wearing only my muslin nightdress and a shawl. He seemed uninterested in me, however, scanning the rooms with his small, dull eyes and rifling through my cupboards, boxes, bins, drawers. Months earlier I had hidden "the bank," Gryffth's hoard of gold coins, in the chimney, but after Junior Mullinax and his brothers tried to rob me I'd left three coins there in a sock and back in December I put my father's watch and the bulk of the coins in a pint jar which I dropped in a five-gallon crock of cooling lard. This crock had a chipped lip but otherwise it looked the same as all the crocks in the storehouse, half-buried in the sawdust floor. Williams discovered the coins in the chimney with little effort, so I was glad of my precautions, and I emptied my box of fairly worthless jewelry—ruby pins, jet combs, and a small pearl brooch—in his open bag with something like gratitude.

We passed the room where Cleo slept with Charlie. The man flung the door open, waiting to hear noises in response. Cleo and I had worked out that if she were caught in the house with Charlie when raiders came she was to play a game with him by hiding underneath the bed. The room was half taken up with sacks of onions and we'd pushed several sacks under the cot to provide cover. This is where she must have lain, clutching the baby to her. I wasn't much worried they'd hurt my boy, but Cleo is a good-looking woman and light-skinned. I remembered what had happened to Nerissa back at Valois and I wanted to prevent it if I could. No sound came from the room, although we could hear men shouting in the yard and a pig squealing.

Now the larder, he said, pushing me ahead. And see if you can't find more money in the flour.

I emptied all the canisters of flour, rice, and tea, with Yellow Teeth growing impatient and reaching over my head to pull down boxes and jars. There was already a terrible mess to clean up. He was angry not to find more gold. Where's the whiskey, then, he shouted, smashing jars of pickles on the floor. I showed him the "dispensary" in the grain bin and he snatched out the single bottle, frowning. There are ten bottles of muscadine wine under the staircase, I told him. I made it myself, so it's not the best tasting. But it's alcohol.

He pulled the cork out of my father's Tennessee mash and took a long swig, leaning close to me in the dim larder. Now I could see what I had been too confused to notice at first: the cuffs of his belted jacket. Holding the bottle to his mouth, the dirty buff-colored facing of his right cuff nearly touched my cheek. As he drank, I noticed that the facing was torn and separating from the sleeve. Underneath the newer piece of fabric was the original red facing, the color of artillery soldiers. He might have been a Confederate soldier who deserted, or he might have been a shirker and a thief who stole the uniform off a dead artilleryman, but he was not a cavalry lieutenant.

You should let me mend your cuff while you're stopping, I said as neutrally as I knew how. Whoever stitched that facing for you didn't know what she was about.

He lowered the bottle and turned his wrist to see the cuff, his small eyes comprehending slowly. He set the bottle on the cupboard and leaned his body forward, pressing me against the drawer. When he did, there was no mistaking how my insolence affected him.

I am not in such a hurry that I can't teach you a lesson, he said, his bumpy face glistening. When I'm done, you will be smarter for the lesson but you will not be so smart-mouthed. Your husband will like to pin a medal on me for it.

Martha

HIS MOUTH WAS SO CLOSE TO MINE THAT HE COULD HAVE bitten off my nose, however, his mouth was not the part of him that worried me. He had pinned me against the cupboard so securely that if I could have lifted both feet in the air at that moment I should not have slipped an inch. Unable to move, I felt his hand lifting my gown. The louvered door behind him opened. Bob filled the doorway. Behind him, Winthrop's tall frame squeezed forward, and Felix, short and broad, pushed into the foreground. All three must have entered the house through the shed-room laundry, the door that faced the kitchen and the woods beyond. I have never been so happy to see anyone in my life as I was to see those men.

The lieutenant is looking for wine, I told them. Help him to load the bottles on his horse.

IT SEEMED TOO BRIGHT in the yard after the larder. I held my hand to my eyes to make out the horsemen and their mounts. One of them had swapped his worn-out nag for our white mare who grazed in the pasture. Their sacks were strapped to the saddles, bulging with my hard-won meat, my wine, my family silver.

The nigger, too, said Yellow Teeth, and Davey looked to me. I stammered but I couldn't find the words. The horseman with the red beard hoisted my poultry boy up before him on the saddle, lashing his hands quickly and tightly to the pommel. They're still paying for slaves in Charlotte, the lieutenant said to me before mounting his horse. But don't look for us there. We don't stay anywhere long. He signaled the others.

Davey! I called. The poor boy twisted in the saddle, crying.

They rode out of the yard, chickens squawking from the bags.

Uriah persists in hovering
near us, at the dinner party

W<small>E ARE STILL CLEANING UP THE MESSES AND DOING A</small> thorough accounting of the losses, and while it is not as bad as I had feared in the proportion of things stolen to things retained it is the loss of certain things of great value that is hard to overcome.

Davey had been of very significant use at Holland Creek and we all feel his absence keenly, Charlie especially. The child wailed terribly when he trotted out to the porch these past two mornings to meet Davey coming up with the eggs and had to be brought in again. I told Cleo to take him down to the henhouse herself and make a game of it. It bothered me greatly that not only had I been powerless to aid a young man who relied on me for his protection but that he had possessed even less power to help himself. His life was not his own, not even to save. The injustice of it rankles even more than the anxiety over what they might have done with him, and that is considerable.

As soon as the "cavalrymen" left I sent Felix to the magistrate's with a report of the raid and of Davey's abduction, but when Captain Mitchell visited yesterday to get a full accounting he had little information to provide and could promise no effective action. No one else in Holland Crossroads has reported an incident like ours, but an elderly planter in West Anchor was hung over a fence and beaten nearly to death when he refused to tell three men on horseback where his gold was buried. There are no lawmen left in the countryside to chase these raiders down, the magistrate explained. Every able-bodied man between the ages of seventeen and forty-seven is off at war, and the scoundrels know it. They can carry out their crimes with impunity, and that includes causing mayhem and stealing property of all kinds.

Abner drove the bulk of the sheep into the woods before Yellow Teeth and his men arrived, so we have been rounding them up for the last two days, finding three lambs in the process. Some continue to straggle home on their own. One of our pigs, the pregnant sow, appeared in the Byars' corn, so I have asked them to keep her when the litter comes and pick two shoats for their trouble. Cleo crawled out from under the bed with Charlie, giving a full report of his obedience in staying silent with her behind the onion sacks. He was rewarded with apple pancakes and cream in recognition of his valor. Achilles was gone so long that day I had almost begun to wonder if he had bolted, but at sundown I heard Cherry Pie's cowbell as she led her pack of refugees home to the barn: Rachel, the second cow, lowing in pain with a full udder, the draft horse, Fly, and Achilles riding Sadie bareback with two hams draped across his shoulders.

I SENSE THAT ABNER is growing jealous of Achilles, perhaps because the latter is consistently resourceful when I need it, especially in his duties as a hostler and cowherd, which Abner has always viewed as his domain. For the sake of preserving harmony, therefore, I refrained from praising Achilles overly much for returning with our draft animals and our small stock of dairy cows intact. Instead, I made sure Cleo fed him and I told Abner to do the milking, telling him he has a way with testy cows.

I fall into captivity

AFTER DEBATING WHETHER OR NOT TO GROW COTTON THIS year I have decided we will cultivate a few acres in case the war ends by October and there are buyers again. The men prepared the ground over the last two days and we will seed tomorrow if it does not rain.

In the afternoon Floyd Parris drove his buggy into the yard, having heard from Captain Mitchell of our predatory visitors. He asked me more than once if I was all right; if it is certain that the false cavalrymen did not "insult" me. I did not tell him more than what I knew he could tolerate well—namely that my servants stood by me and scared the men off before any assaults against my virtue could be carried out. In truth I am changed by the event, and not for the better. Seeing how easily I can be physically overpowered has sapped a great deal of my fighting spirit. In the wake of this violation of my home and my person I experience an unfamiliar emotion: fear. I perceive that fear rushes into the spaces left when confidence flees, when a woman realizes that she is no longer a person of any particular importance or authority, as she had long been allowed to believe. It has tipped the balance of the world in an uncanny way.

As he was leaving, Floyd insisted that I join him and Agnes and a few guests in Laurens in three days' time, when there will be a dinner party. It is to celebrate Nolan Oglesby's engagement to a young lady from Charleston and also to observe the Parrises' wedding anniversary.

And yours, as well, Floyd observed, yours and the major's.

I know he is trying to be kind and to take my mind off our plight here at Holland Creek but the thought of celebrating engagements and anniversaries when I have not laid eyes on my own husband in nearly a year strikes me as unutterably dreary. Floyd did his best to talk me into it, pledging to send Junius to fetch me and working out with Cleo that she will bring Charlie and accompany me in order to visit her mother, who cooks for a neighbor in Laurens. Eventually I agreed, mostly to give Cleo a visit with her mother.

Before he drove away Floyd chucked Charlie under the chin and then bent to pat Gopher, the timid guard dog he gave me. Did she play her part? he asked, and looking at her beat her tail against the porch floor I hadn't the heart to say anything but that she is good with the child. Hello, what's this, said Floyd, pulling Gryffth's revolver out of a pile of decaying leaves behind the mock orange. It must have fallen out of red-beard's pants when he was struggling to tie Davey to the saddle, and in the hubbub of that morning the thieves had overlooked it. As had we.

This small recovery offers me a good deal of relief. With the Colt restored, I feel more comfortable in my decision not to write to Gryffth about the invaders. Having heard how we are preyed upon, he will feel responsible, but will be powerless to help when he is so far away. I fear a distraction of that magnitude could prove deadly for him. It is a risk I dare not take.

We are disturbed
in our cookery

I FOLLOWED THE MEN OUT TO THE EASTERN FIELD THIS MORN-
ing to supervise the cotton planting. They put their seed sacks
over their shoulders and walked into the rising sun. Not wanting to rile Bob, who is sensitive about questions touching on his
expertise, I nevertheless asked him if it was absolutely necessary
to sow the ginned seed so thickly on the rows—if we might not
make a bit of money selling our excess sacks for oil.

Penny wise, yes'm, but pound foolish, Bob replied. "One for
the rook" and so forth.

One for the what, I asked. I did not understand the term.

One for the rook, Missus. One for the crow. One to die. One
to grow. Most of these seeds will never be cotton plants—that's
the law of things. It's the lucky devil who lives. And he went
back to his planting.

I find Mr. Barkis
"going out with the tide"

Aᴮɴᴇʀ ʀᴇᴛᴜʀɴᴇᴅ ғʀᴏᴍ ᴛʜᴇ ᴄʀᴏssʀᴏᴀᴅs ᴛʜɪs ᴍᴏʀɴɪɴɢ with two letters for me, one bearing good tidings and one with bad.

The good letter was from Aunt Florie, containing snippets of news from her life in Chesterfield County, where she removed to a rented cottage when the situation in the low country grew too unsettled and work on her Summerville house was suspended. She spends a good deal of time with dear Mildred and Baby Roe; I envy them both.

In her note she apologized for her oversight in neglecting to forward the enclosed letter from my husband, the one that caught up with her in Cheraw in January. I opened Gryffth's letter and set out each one of the three sheets on the table where I could view them individually. The thrill of seeing his writing incapacitated my comprehension; it took several minutes before I could focus productively enough to read and understand what he communicated. He told my aunt about their winter camp, about the snug huts they built beside the Rapidan. He wrote that he would appreciate her mailing him a box of apples, a ham if she can spare it, some twists of tobacco, and a bottle of brandy as soon as possible—that all the brigade has to eat is cornpone, hardtack, and moldy bacon, with his men joking that the bacon "outranks" General Hill. (My aunt wrote me that she sent all to him by way of Gibsonville on the C&S railroad as instructed, but worried it would not arrive intact, based on the reports of her women friends with loved ones in other companies, whose boxes were pilfered before they arrived.) He wrote that the Union's Fifth Corps have made their winter camp a few miles away at Brandy Station. It gives a fellow a cold feeling, he said, to know that so many men we have met before in battle are now playing checkers and washing their underwear upwind of us, passing the time before the weather warms and we can all resume our full-time occupation of trying to slaughter one another. I have copied out the last page of his letter here, because it summons his voice so vividly every time I read it:

I heard from a soldier here at camp, a lieutenant from Tomahawk County, that Mr. Fincher died suddenly in September. My wife would have been on her way to Raleigh (or leaving it) when he took ill, I reckon. I do regret Mr. Quincey's passing, as he was ever the most scrupulous and decent gentleman to me, and the bestowal of his blessing on my marriage to his daughter was more than I deserved. I worry about how this news has affected my darling girl. Was she very downcast at the funeral? Have you seen or talked to her since then? Since I heard of his death my conscience has been troubling me greatly, or maybe it is due to a general lowering of spirits as this war drags on, but I often feel I did wrong to claim Placidia for my own. It was perhaps the most selfish thing I have done. No one can say I do not love her. I love her more than I did when I kissed her good-bye two days after our wedding. But loving is not the same as providing and protecting, which is a husband's role. I used to think I was playing that role in Lee's army. I'm not as sure of that anymore. Please remember her to me and ask her to keep writing.

I touch the words *darling girl* and imagine he can feel that touch, in his camp beside the river. I am so afraid his love won't last until the war is over.

Mr. Peggotty and
Mrs. Steerforth

Meanwhile, the bad letter is from my stepmother, Mrs. Fincher, notifying me that the servants at Valois are soon to be dispersed. Father's will expressed his hope of keeping servants' families together "if fiscally feasible" but was not specific about the course to be followed if it were not. With Aunt Florie's guidance we sold off fifty acres of timber and leased a good deal of cleared land to the neighbors; one hundred head of cattle and Father's hunters, Caesar and Cannonball, were auctioned, as was some of the furniture, which will go towards settling debts and paying taxes. We were lucky to sell that much, considering how few solvent buyers remain in Tomahawk County. But the fate of the human property has been contended without resolution.

Carthene allowed my aunt to take Mercy and her son Ephraim, although not without some arm-twisting and, I imagine, a significant number of gold coins slipped into Carthene's hands. She maintains, with some basis in truth, that despite the fact that she does not truly "own" any of the property at Valois except what Father specifically bequeathed her, she must continue to manage and maintain it as long as she lives there, and claims that she cannot make the plantation successful without a certain number of skilled servants remaining on the estate. She insists that she has my interests at heart in her planned division of the remaining labor pool—diverting certain servants to neighbors and traders who are paying a "fair" price to the estate that is in my name. I am uncomfortable contemplating the separations that will have to be endured, particularly in Nerissa's large family and that of the field boss, Calhoun, whose grandparents were acquired by my grandfather decades ago and whose descendants have lived on the estate ever since. What cannot be denied is that the state of the farm's finances requires drastic action.

Her letter took eight days to reach me and the "dispersal" is scheduled for the day after tomorrow. All the servants deemed by Carthene to be nonessential, and they number more than thirty, will be gathered in the yard and grouped in two rings which are to be marked out with lime dust and designated as "Field/Stables" or "House." She writes that Abner will be allowed to stay with me after all, in accordance with Q.V.'s wishes, but that if I require any additional servants I must come to Valois on the scheduled date or send an emissary to bid for those hands needed at Holland Creek. She adds, unnecessarily, that in consideration of the estate's urgent need of cash, no family members will be permitted to hold out, gratis, "any negroes who may generate a reasonable offer from a third party."

The entire tone of her letter is revolting in its synthesis of feigned concern for my interests and sham objectivity as regards her own (and those of her acquisitive Oglesby relations), but practically I am not in a position to oppose it. I do not plan to return to Valois for this sad event, especially as I can offer no alternative to banishment for those servants facing it and I dread the thought of deferring to my stepmother on this issue or clashing with her when deference fails.

My Aunt astonishes me

THIS MORNING I BEGAN MAKING PREPARATIONS FOR TRAVEL-ing to Laurens tomorrow, and while fetching my carpet bag Abner surprised me by introducing the topic of the sale at Valois. It is a marvelous fact that the servants spread and receive news on their own mysterious grapevines far faster and more efficiently than their masters do, despite lacking literacy, and Abner has already gained detailed intelligence of the dispersal taking place at Valois on Saturday. He told me he is grateful for the chance to stay at Holland Creek and continue his duties here (where he no doubt appreciates my management style, a far less disciplined variety than that wielded by Mrs. Fincher). However, he believes that I am in great need of a *second woman* on the farm, especially as Cleo is only on loan from the Parris household. A strong young woman, he claims, one who cooks capably, cleans, looks after poultry and small animals, tends the kitchen garden and *weaves*—meaning that she could help to generate income with the acquisition of a loom—would benefit me and help the farm to prosper.

I already knew the answer before asking the question but because I admired how skillfully Abner had constructed this persuasive argument for bringing his sweetheart to Holland Creek, I asked: Do you have a candidate in mind?

Nerissa, he responded with a radiant smile.

I hadn't the heart to tell Abner that I cannot afford Nerissa, whose many skills, docile nature, youth, and light-skinned, appealing appearance will no doubt generate competing bids at Carthene's event. Instead, I told him that I would consider it, and when, an hour later, he broached the subject again, knowing that I will be in Laurens when the dispersal takes place, I took pity on him and drafted a letter to my stepmother making an offer of 500 Confederate dollars for Nerissa, which I cannot afford. (Before the war, she would have fetched more than twice that.) I told Abner he may take the nag left by the robber-cavalryman, the only horse Bob can spare (and we cannot truly spare Abner, with so much planting to do between now and the end of May) and he may ride tomorrow for Valois as soon as Cleo and I have departed and he has tended to the stock. I gave him the bid and a pass for the patrollers and wished him good luck, but I suspect he will come home disappointed.

*Mr. Wickfield and his
partner wait upon my Aunt*

April 15, 1864

J UNIUS ARRIVED WITH THE BUGGY TO CONVEY US TO LAURENS.
Cleo and I dashed around the house handing Charlie off to one
another as we hurried to finish packing. I have no decent dresses
left which are suitable for a dinner party among cultured people,
but I have kept my wedding dress, the blue taffeta, folded in a
sheet in the blanket chest. Cleo helped me smooth the wrinkles
and told me I would suit, although I have lost weight and the
dress hangs on me.

As we climbed into the buggy with our bags, the child, his
blankets, and his painted horse, Abner approached, his face flashing fire. It is too low, he said, thrusting the letter at me.

What kind of insolence is this, I said, losing my patience with
the lovesick hostler.

It is too low what you offer, he repeated. It will be outbid.

I know Abner does not read or write. Nor does Cleo, Bob,
or any of the field hands. Who read this to you? I snatched the
letter from him.

Achilles, he said.

I was too surprised to speak.

He says, You have bid 500. You know it will not buy Nerissa.

I was so furious that I jumped down from the buggy, ripping
my taffeta as I did, and marched off to the barn where Achilles

can be found most mornings cleaning out the stalls. Achilles! I shouted. He looked up from the muck. Is it true? Do you read and write? He stared at me, trying to read my face. Is it true?

Yes, ma'am, he said after a moment.

Why didn't you tell me when you came here?

I wasn't sure you would think it a good thing, miss.

Who taught you? Was it the Wilkersons?

Something like a smile crossed his face.

No, miss. Ma taught me. Her mistress taught her.

His smile vanished, and when it did I realized he hadn't been smiling after all but had risked an acutely subtle expression of pride.

He said, I hope I haven't done wrong in telling Abner what you wrote.

I was trying to collect the few facts Achilles had provided about his mother, about his beginnings.

You said your mother carried you off the place where you were born. Why would she do that if the mistress was teaching her letters? If she was kind to her?

He pushed a shovelful of manure away from my embroidered slippers.

She was kind at first. That's what my mother said. But it changed when I was born. Then it weren't no good.

How did it change?

The missus made the master sell her, and me with her. A wagon took us across the river and we never went back.

I could not take my eyes off Achilles' face, the lapis-blue eyes set in smooth brown stone, like the polished mask of a god in a Greek tragedy. Of course I knew those eyes. And the broad back, which tilts to the left when he is bending to some work with purpose. And the manner in which his lips draw back in silence, well before the laughter comes (although Achilles laughs much less than his progenitor). It had been my vanity protecting me from seeing this, my overgrown pride in being Quincey Valois Fincher's child. I chose blindness over truth, like any woman in my position would have done.

Mr. Micawber delivers some valedictory remarks

THE BIG PLACE WHERE YOU STARTED OUT, I SAID. WHERE THE missus taught your mother. (My voice was stretched so thin I had to repeat the question.) The place where you started out. Does the river cut through to the south? Is there a grove of giant pecans shading the lane to the house?

He didn't answer right away, but eventually he nodded. That's right. The river always tops its banks in spring.

Do you know the name of this place?

The sigh, like steam escaping. Relief, or resignation. *Valois, miss. It was a long time ago.*

I stood looking at this man. I wished I could go back to seeing him as I had in the weeks before this moment arrived, before knowledge was dropped on me like a dead limb breaking from a tree. But I could not. In the hushed way Achilles had spoken to me of Valois, handing it over wiped clean of any inflection, of any value, I understood that the limb had dropped on him long before striking me, perhaps as far back as the clearing in the pignuts and the first sight of the major's bride come all the way from that far-off realm. He had been protecting the knowledge, even as he made use of it. I could not fathom what our shared bloodline meant to him, but it made me dizzy as the implications rushed in.

I longed to unburden myself to someone, then. I wanted someone to give truthful answers to my questions. I felt like a child who has been playing an elaborate game for the longest time and believes that she has almost mastered it, only to discover that it is an illusion: that there are grown-ups toiling behind the scenes to keep the pantomime in play, cheating to make it so. Continuation depends upon all cruelty and complexity being concealed from us children, allowing us our fictions while preserving our state of idiocy. It is all a rotten business.

I marched back to the buggy and climbed in, not seeing or hearing the chatter of people around me beyond knowing that everyone wanted me to tell them what was happening next. I saw Abner standing at the horse's flank, watching me, and I thrust the letter at him. Go or stay, do whatever suits you, I heard myself say in a tone of such venomous coldness that my son swiveled his head to stare at me. It is not in my hands and never has been.

Abner's face collapsed. I poked Junius to be started and we rolled out of the yard at a fast clip, with Charlie whimpering and my heart clenched in pain. It was not an auspicious departure.

*Traddles makes a figure
in Parliament and I
report him*

WHILE THE PARRIS HOME ON HARPER STREET IS NOT NEARLY
as grand as my childhood home, I have grown so unaccustomed
to well-lit, high-ceilinged rooms furnished in elegant style that
I felt like a mud-hen set down in a palace. At table we were: my
stepsister Agnes and her husband Floyd, my stepbrother Nolan and
his fiancée, Miss Willetta Hammond, a Mr. and Mrs. Lipscomb,
he an engineer and Commissioner of Roads and Bridges for the
district, and a Mr. Covington, who is a chemistry professor at
the college in Columbia and does something for the government.
Being so distracted by the day's events and so dazzled by crystal
and candles, I forgot to note what we were eating, although I
heard Miss Hammond refer to the "vermicelli soup" and Mr.
Covington made mention of the quail. I almost laughed imagining
the company's reaction if I were to tell them that the last meal I
consumed was rabbit hash.

My stepbrother has matured considerably in the past year,
filling out and growing a set of blond whiskers. His manners are
improved, along with his appearance, and he no longer resembles
the reckless boy who created such mischief at his sister's wedding reception. Miss Hammond is pretty but lacks depth—she
spoke at length of the social events that have been disrupted in

Charleston but demonstrated little grasp of the reasons for the inconvenience. Meanwhile, Mrs. Lipscomb talked incessantly of the problems her husband has had with the impressment law diverting negroes from essential road-building projects to work on military fortifications and railroad beds. She claims the men are fed poorly by the army and worked nearly to death, after which they are returned to their owners in no condition to be useful.

On the long drive here I was so rattled by the revelations made by Achilles and so confused by my own responses to that information that I hardly knew how I was going to rise to this social occasion. In the end, the rest of the company was mostly content to let me be reticent, ascribing it to an inclination to honor my husband in his absence with discretion. To that end they filled my silences with banter and engaged me without demanding too much of me. Some difficulty with the servants had put Agnes in a bad humor, because she was very short in her responses to friendly inquiries at table and frequently excused herself to retire to the pantry, where loud whispering could be heard. I was shocked when Sukie, whom I had tolerated only briefly at Holland Creek, appeared at my side serving the soup. Thanks to Floyd I was not wholly unprepared. She would not catch my eye, but Agnes regarded me sharply as Sukie moved about the dining room, and I found that unsettling.

After reminding the company that Major Hockaday was away in Virginia serving his country in Lee's Army, and after leading a toast to my husband's health and to the courageous boys of the Brockman Guards, Floyd related the story of my household's plundering by bandit-cavalrymen. This generated a good deal of excited conversation and questions which I would rather not have fielded, especially once they learned that I had been disarmed by the leader and that three of my field hands had spared me from greater indignities.

I would have drawn and quartered the fellow! Mr. Covington kept repeating to the assembly. Hanging's too good for that sort!

Mr. Lipscomb also became quite animated at this point, narrating in lurid detail the story of a man in Anderson who sold his cotton crop one morning and whose head was split open with an axe while he slept that night. The murderers stole his profits—$1,000 in gold—before melting into the forest. Everyone agreed these were dark times we lived in, and Mr. Covington warned Nolan to arm himself well for his journey to Tennessee when he sets out tomorrow.

The Wanderer

Mrs. Lipscomb asked Nolan what he could be thinking of, riding unaccompanied to eastern Tennessee at a time like this, when a rogue's gallery of Union commanders and their columns had nearly pounded the mountains flat converging on Chattanooga the previous November, occupying the city, routing our men at Lookout Mountain and chasing Bragg back to Georgia. And if anyone needed reminding, she told us how W. T. Sherman, that red-headed, asthmatic demoniac who commands the Army of the Tennessee and who, it is rumored, sleeps only in his saddle and is sustained by nothing more than sardine sandwiches and cheap cigars, had driven his bluecoats double-quick through the icy mountain passes to Knoxville, forcing Longstreet to raise the siege of Fort Sanders. His division forded the Little Tennessee with a bridge made from the homes they'd sacked in Morgantown. Ask them at Maryville and Cleveland, at the burned-out ironworks in Tellico and all along the Memphis-Charleston rail-lines, if you dare. Those Tennesseans will tell you that no southerner is safe in that corner of the country.

Nolan listened calmly as Mrs. Lipscomb regaled us with her jeremiad of disastrous Cumberland campaigns, the corner of his mouth creased in a knowing smile. His cheerful expression did not quite project arrogance but rather intimated that, like some Achaean warrior from the *Iliad*, he was certain of the gods' support, and on the basis of their inevitable humiliation, he pitied any countrymen who doubted victory over Troy. (No one questioned why Nolan was not fighting to bring this goal to fruition, taking it for granted, apparently, that the senior Oglesbys were too well-bred to allow one of their own to muck about as a common soldier).

When Mrs. Lipscomb paused to catch her breath, he spoke up, observing that there was, undeniably, a threading-the-needle aspect to the undertaking, but that nothing of value was gained without risk. He claimed to be well-prepared for the journey and said he did not need a strong servant to accompany him as he knew the southern Smokies like he knew the streets of Charleston. He told us his grandparents' overseer was riding to meet him in Dahlonega where they would collect their first small party of a dozen negroes working at the sawmill his grandfather owned on the Chestatee River. He and Mr. Mahaffey would ride together through the mountains at Cooper's Gap, where unionists and Union pickets were thick on the ground, bringing the negroes to the main farm in McMinn County, Tennessee. Here fifty more men and women waited to be hauled in wagons south to Alabama before heading westward into southern Mississippi and Louisiana. Skirting Union lines with the help of a sympathetic federal commander known to Nolan, the servants would be smuggled across the river into Texas. Nolan's grandfather had already purchased a saltworks there and his grandmother had gone ahead to make the house ready.

Isn't this "refugeeing" very dangerous business, asked Mr. Lipscomb, who sounded skeptical. Risking your life to hang on to a few dozen negroes?

We're protecting them as much as we're preserving our livelihood, Nolan answered. Where would they live if we didn't provide it? How would they eat? What would they do? My grandparents take their responsibilities very seriously. All the Oglesbys do.

Yes, but in any case those questions will be answered when . . . Here Mrs. Lipscomb must have kicked Mr. Lipscomb under the table, because the engineer gave a yelp mid-sentence and closed his mouth. I knew what he was going to say. We all did. "When we lose the war" is how he was going to complete his sentence. Next to me, my stepbrother's fiancée began to cry.

*Traddles and I in
conference with the
Misses Spenlow*

I DIDN'T KNOW THE MOUNTAINS WERE SO DANGEROUS, MISS
Hammond whimpered. Nolan's kept all that to himself.

Quite, Mr. Covington chimed in. He seemed to be acquiring a
plummy British accent as the evening wore on and his consump-
tion of alcohol increased.

He said, I knew a chap signed on with the Thomas Legion,
extraordinary company made up of white men and Cherokee
Indians, they were crossing the Oconaluftee Turnpike going from
North Carolina into Tennessee. A sniper fired from the brush
and the shot came so close to this bloke's body that the smoke
was trapped in his coat and boiled out his collar! But the bullet
missed—lucky devil! Not a scratch on him.

I felt a slight wavering in my bloodstream that might have
been the wine or might have been the words, but I looked up
and saw Floyd staring back at me with true concern on his face.

Floyd said, let's change the subject, shall we gentlemen? We'll
give the ladies nightmares. He maneuvered the men on to the
porch with the promise of cigars and brandy. Meanwhile, Agnes
invited the ladies to join her in the parlor, without much enthusiasm, it seemed. As I ducked into the hallway to fetch my wrap,
Floyd appeared at my side, asking if I was well. I told him I'd
felt faint only briefly, thinking of the major's close brushes with
death in the years he had been at war and the bullets he had yet to

face before I would have him home again. It sometimes seemed impossible to me that he could survive it.

Damned nuisance, that chemist, Floyd said. I don't know him as well as I thought I did, or I wouldn't have asked him to dinner.

I assured him I wasn't offended by anything Mr. Covington had said or anyone else had said, for that matter, but I did wonder if Agnes was troubled by something? Had *I* given offense?

Floyd made a noise of exasperation. Not you, he answered. Agnes seems to think we don't have enough servants in Laurens, as if six house servants in a town home in wartime could be considered roughing it!

She wants Cleo back, I said.

He hesitated, looking over his shoulder and lowering his voice. She's not getting her back. Cleo told me how attached she has grown to Charles, and to you. She grew up working for my parents and my younger brother's family at Coldwater and is happier with a simpler, more rustic way of life. When my brother Neill moved to Alabama I brought her here because I knew how good a child-minder she was and I was hoping her presence would encourage Agnes to endeavor a bit harder . . .

He blushed. That Agnes and I could start our family. But with or without Cleo, that hasn't happened.

I touched Floyd's arm, appreciating how considerate he has been on my behalf and Charlie's. At that moment Agnes stepped into the hall from the parlor and locked her eyes on the two of us, freezing us in position.

Yes, Agnes? Floyd called in a cool voice, refusing to be cowed.

I believe you'd be better entertained in the parlor with the rest of us, Agnes said to me, without the pretense of cordiality.

I am Married

WE GATHERED ON SETTEES PULLED NEAR THE FIRE, AS THE night had turned chilly. A young servant with terrified eyes served us cups of punch before scurrying out of the parlor. Talk quickly turned to the subject of children, as it so often does in feminine gatherings of this sort. Mrs. Lipscomb has a new grandchild and lectured us on teething remedies while Agnes scowled. Ignoring her, Mrs. Lipscomb turned to me, saying, I understand Mrs. Parris's girl Cleo is helping you with your own baby out at Holland Creek?

My heart lifted for the first time that night. Charles is a delight, I told her. Bright, ravenous, and running everywhere. He keeps Cleo and me on our toes.

How extraordinary, the lady marveled. How can he be "running" at such a young age?

Agnes looked pleased, at last. Not so young, she told the women. Charles Hockaday is twenty-eight months old.

But . . . I thought . . . Mrs. Lipscomb stammered. I understood that you and the major were married last April, the day after Mr. and Mrs. Parris celebrated their nuptials.

You're correct, I answered, forcing myself to smile. Charles is Gryffth's son by his first wife, who died from typhoid fever in '62. Gryffth was on the march with his brigade for much of that year and couldn't obtain leave until it was too late. He was home for several weeks nursing Charlie back to health.

Agnes leaned over to Miss Hammond and said under her breath, but loudly enough for all of us to hear: *That's Mama's baby, Daddy's maybe.*

I might have been able to convince myself that I had misheard, if the idiotic Miss Hammond had not giggled. Mrs. Lipscomb's stricken expression helped to confirm the insult. She did not laugh.

I stood, not knowing what I was going to say. Miss Hammond looked up at me and stopped giggling.

Agnes, I began. My stepsister watched me, eyes narrowed, taking in the ripped hem of my skirt. I swallowed my considerable anger, surprised to discover that what remained was a pit of black, airless, soul-rending loneliness. I thought of Gryffth's mouth on my neck, his laughter shaking the bed. Can one die of loneliness, I asked myself? I thought I heard the first Mrs. Hockaday's voice in my head, saying: *I did.*

I am not amiable company tonight, I said aloud. The shock from the robbery is proving harder to dispel than I expected, and I have a headache of epic proportions. Could I impose on you and Mr. Parris to allow Junius to drive me home?

What, tonight? Agnes exclaimed. Floyd assured me you were staying through the weekend.

I couldn't trust myself to speak so I shook my head, hoping she would have mercy.

You really don't look well, poor dear, Mrs. Lipscomb said, coming to my aid.

I must decline, Sister, said Agnes, cutting short Mrs. Lipscomb's show of charity. We are all having breakfast and seeing Nolan off to Tennessee in the morning. Afterwards we are riding to church in the carriage, so I will want my servant and my horses to be fresh for the drive.

Our Housekeeping

I STUDIED AGNES. SEEING HER SATISFACTION IN THIS MOMENT helped me to understand something about her that I had been too innocent or stupid to comprehend before, despite my cousin's and my aunt's best efforts to teach me. Agnes Oglesby was jealous of me. She was far superior to me in terms of material wealth, in education, in breeding. She was married to a charming, good-hearted man who kept her company every day. And yet she envied me (for what, I couldn't have testified in a court of law!) and because of that she was frightened of me and of the power I held over her. It was a power I hadn't known I wielded, but in my newfound appreciation of its existence I perceived that nothing Agnes valued was held in high regard by me. That was the injury I caused her as well as the leverage I brandished.

If she had known how much assurance I lacked about my own place in the cosmos or the pain I felt about my father after hearing Achilles' revelations that morning, it might have bolstered her confidence. In any case, it was clear that I did not belong in this parlor, tonight, with these people. But the thought that followed immediately was that I did not know if I truly belonged anywhere.

Forgive me, Sister, I told her, but I am determined to sleep in my own bed tonight. If you will not send Junius, I will walk to the livery stable and try to secure a horse before the grooms have gone to sleep. I gathered my shawl about me, realizing I would have to sacrifice the carpet bag. I said, please let Cleo know I will be back with Abner on Monday to bring her and Charlie home. I walked out of the parlor, startling the timid girl who stood in the hall, holding a silver tray bigger than she was. Back door? I asked. She pointed. I passed through a labyrinth of service rooms, finally finding a door that led to the garden. In trying to make my escape across the lawn, however, my pale shawl must have caught the attention of one of the men on the front porch, all of whom began *halloo*-ing me like a pack of schoolboys. I paused at the privet hedge, where Floyd caught up with me, wanting to know where I was running to.

I explained, feeling more composed now that I had made a plan of action, and all the more determined. Floyd was not pleased to hear that Agnes had declined my request for a ride back to Holland Creek. The other men came down off the porch and stood tapping their cigars into the shrubbery.

Mrs. Hockaday, I would be honored to drive you home in my buggy, Mr. Covington put in, so avidly that he missed sounding chivalrous.

I am her stepbrother, Nolan countered the chemist. If anyone should be escorting her home it should be me. But Parris will have to loan you a pony, he added, turning to me, eyes dazed with brandy. His face was flushed and it made his whiskers appear almost white against his skin.

Floyd ground out his cigar stub with the toe of his boot, asking me, Is this something I can remedy? Can I calm the waters in some way?

Over his shoulder I spied Agnes emerging from the side porch, flashing an expression of enmity mixed with trepidation—a dangerous brew. Whether I was reacting to that troubled expression genuinely, or responding to it with the notion that I could gain the advantage if I grasped it, I cannot say. I can say that upon hearing the tender solicitude in Floyd's voice I had a vivid impression of Gryffth sitting close to me under the swamp rose saying *Falling in love with you was like walking out on a sunny day and being struck by lightning*. His voice in my ear was so strong it nearly cut my heart in two.

I miss my husband, I told Floyd, grimly choking back tears. I miss him. And I want him back.

Mr. Dick fulfills my
Aunt's prediction

FLOYD ENDED ALL DISCUSSION THEN, AS I KNEW HE WOULD. He called for Junius, shooting dark looks at Agnes, and I was only able to persuade him to refrain from driving me back to the farm and to stay and carry out his duties as host by promising to send Junius home to Laurens that night with word that I was safely locked indoors.

Otherwise, we will none of us sleep for care of you, he told me. All the men agreed.

I WAS GLAD OF my escape from that house. The night, while chilly, was pulsing with the promise of spring, the air smelling of sweet mud and new leaves. A whippoorwill called from the beeches when we crossed the river, and about a mile from the farm an enormous owl swooped over the carriage, the wind from his outstretched wings stirring the ribbons on my bonnet.

The most remarkable occurrence of this remarkable night was feeling the first Mrs. Hockaday riding in the carriage with Junius and me all the way home like a silent chaperone, as shadowy as the owl yet imbued with a more substantial essence than I had supposed she possessed. Her presence made me feel unsettled. Restless. As if she were pressing me to step outside the ordinary daylight world and see what lay beyond that, in the shadows.

Hidden. I tightened my shawl around my shoulders and strained to see a lamplight through the trees, any sign we were approaching home. I didn't want to look into her world, perhaps because I know how insubstantial the barrier is between hers and mine, and no one returns from where she dwells.

After sending Junius back to Laurens, after locking the doors at the farmhouse and dousing the lamps, I still felt her. I feel her now. She is standing in the shadows, wanting me to come near. I could so easily do so—that's what makes me afraid.

I thought I would fall into bed as soon as I arrived home, but the house is too quiet and too dark: I cannot sleep. I sit down at the major's desk to relate the day's events to *David Copperfield* and as I write I feel my strength returning. I feel the world of shadows retreating. I feel the cord connecting me to him.

God bless you, Gryffth, in your cabin by the Rapidan or your tent pitched on some blasted field of battle. If I had the whippoorwill's voice I would sing through the night all that weighs on my heart and all that I'm longing for. I would sing until you found your way home to me.

2204 Harbert Ave.,

MEMPHIS,
TENNESSEE

April 25, 1892

Dear Mummy,

I hope you are well in Cheraw and are not worrying
about me. I'm sorry I have not written to you until now;
I wanted to be clear in my understanding of the situation
here before committing any words to paper, and while I
still lack full knowledge of the circumstances it is time
that I communicated some particulars. First, be assured
that Achilles has made my welfare and my reputation his
primary concern during my visit. He arranged for me to
board near the campus with a highly respectable woman,
Mrs. Whiteside, now retired from her position as a professor of geology at one of the women's colleges here.
She introduced me to her three boarders, all individuals
of learning and distinction, and all *women*, mind you,
because she says a household is more orderly that way, a
point of view I know she shares with you.

Achilles dined with us almost every night after his
classes concluded excepting those nights he led tutori-
als. He has proven to be quite popular with everyone in
the household, due partly to his personal magnetism,
a trait you attribute to his mother, but also because of
his natural curiosity about people and human nature in
general. His interest tends to draw out even reticent individuals after they have spent a few minutes conversing

with him. (I can speak to this quality at length because
in dramatic moments of self-recrimination I have convinced myself that this was the means of my undoing.) I
do not mean to imply that he has been flirtatious with Mrs.
Whiteside's boarders—far from it. In fact, at the beginning of my stay he made it touchingly clear that he and I
dwelled on a plane of familiarity and closeness with which
mere affinity could not compete, and the ladies are well-
disposed towards me sufficiently that they honored this
understanding.

One week after I moved into the house on Harbert
Avenue, however, Achilles finally resolved to read the
Dickens book that was his mother's. He warned me of this
one night after my friends had excused themselves and
retired to the parlor with Mrs. Whiteside for a game of
Old Maid and we were alone. He took my hand and told
me that he had resolved to venture on a risky undertaking.
Naturally, I assumed he was going to speak of something
quite different having to do with the two of us, but he
said that he had made up his mind to read Placidia's book
despite the dire warnings you issued. He catalogued his
reasons for me but I confess my mind rambled off to other
topics, confused about how this matter of his long-dead
mother's diary had become such a compelling priority. He
left me that night telling me that I might not see him for
a day or two but in fact it was four days later that he sur-
faced, calling at the house to take me walking.

We walked along the streets of the neighborhood and
all around the campus and eventually came to sit on a
bench outside the library where the lamps were being lit.

It was a beautiful night. The moon was rising through the maples and the air was heavy with the scent of wisteria. I could not enjoy it. That's because as soon as I opened the door to Achilles that night I saw that he was changed. No one who knew him less thoroughly than me would have noticed it—he possessed the same charming ease of manner and still appeared engaged in all the topics of conversation I introduced (and I talked too much that night because I was so conscious of the alteration in him that I did not know how to address it except to banish silence, even blundering into the topic of Valois and the lofty plans we'd made for carrying out social and agricultural reforms there). It was no use. Some key portion of him was absent. Elsewhere.

Knowing the strain he has been under since his father's passing, I asked him if there was anything I could do to restore him to the peace of mind he seemed to enjoy when we spent time together nearly a year ago. He smiled, but there was no mirth in it. He told me that once known, there is nothing that can be *un*known.

I answered that this is precisely where the value lies in acquiring knowledge—it can never be taken from us as other treasures may be. Again, the smile, without warmth, but as if the movement of his mouth caused him pain deep in his body. Exactly, he said. I wish you had reminded me of that fact four days ago.

...

MUMMY, DO YOU EVER think back on Mrs. Hampton's ball in Columbia, the summer I turned nineteen? I could hardly believe it when you and Aunt Nettie told me that

not only would I be allowed to stay up until the early
hours of the morning, but that it was customary for all the
young ladies in the cotillion to dance through the night
and be feted with breakfast the next day. I had never experienced anything so magical before that night—it's possible I never shall. But you said something to me on the ride
back to our hotel the next day that was more memorable
than any of the glittering, transitory pleasures I experienced at the ball. We had been speaking of the young men
who filled my dance card that night, and of one young
man in particular, Preston Farley, whose grandfather
served on the board of Wofford College and whose father
had been in Daddy's regiment. I liked Preston very much
on short acquaintance, and considering the time we chat-
ted and laughed between dances, assumed he liked me
a little.

I was prattling on about him in the carriage and you
said, "Try to be a little less clever in a gentleman's company, Roe. Men fear the hard work that comes from living
alongside a wit."

I didn't believe you at the time, despite the fact that
I never again heard from Mr. Farley. In the weeks and
months that followed the ball, I received invitations from
a few young men to take part in social events, but as I told
you at the time, they were not men who interested me
enough to develop deeper friendships. It was only later,
as I watched my school friends become engaged and married, that I realized you had not spoken to me that night
with the intent to wound, but had been trying to spare me
a lonely life of spinsterhood.

When I met Miss Taylor's brother Elliott two summers ago and we all gathered at the Taylor family's lake house for the regatta, I consciously tempered my natural inclinations to dominate the conversation, or even just to hold my own in an exchange of views, because I felt true affinity for Mr. Taylor and did not want to throw over what I'd grimly begun to view as my best chance for domestic contentment.

Elliott holds conservative views about most things and can be somewhat dull in lively company because of his tendency to express himself in proclamations, implying that his views are the definitive word on the matter and no expanded dialectic is necessary. He can be ponderous, in other words. However, during that week in Creve Coeur I also found him to be kind-hearted in the way he included his younger and older kinsmen in activities he might have held out exclusively to himself, his sister, and their particular guests. In personal conversations, whenever the two of us were left on the sidelines during a sack race or allowed to talk companionably in the library after dinner, I also discovered him to have an excellent sense of humor, telling me self-effacing stories about his Dutch grandmother's intolerance for his antics as a little boy ("Who do you think you are, a little tin god?") and his less-than-stellar prowess as a footballer at Yale.

Much of this you know already. What I did not tell you is that *I have never been in love* with Elliott Taylor—not while I was enjoying his company that summer, nor even during the trip he made to Cheraw with Leonora the following winter. Instead, I persuaded myself that he would

be *enough* for me, Mummy. Do you understand? And I
would have done right by Mr. Taylor if I had accepted his
proposal when Leonora and I returned to St Louis last
May, because the two of us are conscientious, compassionate people who want many of the same things in life.

I would have done right by Mr. Taylor if I had not
made the fatal error of suggesting to his sister that we
stop over in Memphis on our journey upriver to look in
on my cousin Achilles, a man I had last laid eyes on when
Aunt Placidia was alive. (It is worth reminding you that
this notion of a detour originated in a letter *you* wrote to
me, before my friend and I departed Charleston.) Back
then, "'Achey'" was a pimply, sulky boy who preferred
hunting rabbits with his dog to socializing with the rest of
us on the porch at Holland Creek. To say that his transformation was astonishing would be overstating it: while
Achilles has fully inherited the tall physique that was his
father's and has outgrown the pimples, he still bears the
raw-boned air of a country boy, despite his academic's
weeds and his fluency in Latin.

Contrary to what you have claimed whenever you and
I try to navigate discussion on this topic (and before I
parted from you in Cheraw on the last occasion, we fairly
stove our boats on that reef . . .), I was not swept off my
feet at first sight by this man. My romantic feelings for him
only developed as he drew me out, guiding Leonora and
I around the college and town while conducting Socratic
discussions with us on race, class, architecture, commerce,
and religion. We argued about Hume's theory of personal
identity compared to Locke's, God's existence, women's

rights, the transmigration of souls, the tenets of stoicism as Marcus Aurelius interpreted them, and whether or not Shakespeare read Sophocles in translation and stole the critically important concept of *hamartia* from the Greek poet's tragic heroes. (Achilles thinks he did.)

I set aside your "witty" warning to me, Mummy, and engaged freely with my cousin in all these conversations and others, while he drank up my words not with his ears but with his dark, astonishing eyes. He focused these on me as if he could not afford to miss a single word spilling from my lips lest the secret of existence be revealed while he was blowing his nose or paying the hack driver. In these exchanges we veered into topics of such liberality that my poor friend Leonora sometimes blushed and stammered, reminding me that anyone eavesdropping on us would think Achilles and I were radicals of the first order instead of two affectionate kinsmen enjoying the compatibility of our lively minds. I set aside my own restriction on enthusiastically exploring questions of politics, philosophy, history, and literature because I assumed I would be shortly affianced to the man for whom I had successfully subverted my natural affinities for these subjects, and could indulge them one last time with a sympathetic intellect.

This was the trap I set for myself—there was my *hamartia*!—and I fell headfirst into it, with my heart igniting in such a welter of overheated dreams and desires that I initially thought I was afflicted with some ailment, one that inflamed my chest and made my knees turn to water whenever Achilles Hockaday came into view or

even when I held one of his letters in my hand. Here's the
tragic part about it, Mummy, the truly Grecian aspect to
this misadventure: now that my involvement with Achilles
is presenting itself in retrospect, I see that some prescient
part of me was expecting this conclusion all along. I
fooled myself into vulnerability by proceeding as if I
were invulnerable, a scenario sure to attract the mischief
of the gods. They lifted me on wings of golden bliss and
dropped me on a desert isle. Hubris. That is the second
lesson Sophocles taught us. Here, then, is my denouement:

Achilles walked me home from the campus that night,
making no attempt to reassure me that the alteration in his
spirits and his behavior was anything less than a permanent effect of reading his mother's wartime diary.

The next day we were due to ride the streetcar out to
Sixteenth Avenue once his classes concluded, to hear a
concert at the Fisk Freed Colored School. When the door-
bell rang, however, there was a messenger boy with a letter from "Professor" Hockaday. He wrote that he wasn't
keeping his appointment that day and that he wouldn't
be calling the next day, either. (His written voice was as
distinctly altered as his actual voice, with all infusions of
wit and warmth drained from it.) He told me that even as
I read this letter he was traveling on a train to Philadelphia, going to look for someone who, if still alive, shared
his name and possibly something more. He wrote that the
envelope enclosed within his letter to me was to be mailed
on to you—it contained the final few dated entries from
his mother's copy of *David Copperfield* extending over
several illustrations, pages he tore from the book while

waiting at the station. He said these entries constituted a *de profundis* of the most unexpected nature, a litany of crimes compounding one another for abhorrence, all narrated in his mother's fervently expressive voice but unsuitable for all readers save He who reads from the Book of Life and makes the Final Judgment. He cautioned that I was not, under any condition, to open the sealed envelope and read the pages. (This hurt me, I confess, because he knows me well enough, or so I thought, that he should not have instructed me like a child to observe the sanctity of a sealed letter addressed to someone other than myself, even if that someone else is my own mother.) I expected there to be more in the letter of a personal nature, and considering that there was none, I understand that he may not be exaggerating the disturbing power of the material.

I found Mrs. Whiteside in the parlor that afternoon, and as she was alone, and as she resembles you slightly, Mother, being a sensitive person capable of very nuanced perceptions but also a straightforward realist, grounded in actualities (you see I've made a pun about geology), I was compelled to ask her advice.

She asked me if Achilles and I had formally exchanged pledges of engagement, either verbally or in writing, and I was forced to answer that we had not. She seemed to take this fact under serious consideration, remaining silent for several long moments, and then she surprised me by switching the subject to the public health. She told me that summer is traditionally an unhealthy season in Memphis due to the yellow fever epidemics that plagued the city not long ago. She pointed out that these infestations are much less severe now that the new water system has been installed but all the same most people who have any means however slender leave town by June or July, and that in fact she closes the house every year on June 15 and goes to stay with her married sister in Lexington. The other boarders are leaving when the term ends in the second week of May, she told me, and won't be back until September. So if you are asking me to put myself in your mother's place or to put myself in Mr. Hockaday's place (and yes, Mrs. Whiteside observed gently, I noticed a marked change in that young man on his last visit to the house) I feel I can anticipate, with confidence, that both of them, if asked, would recommend that you return to South Carolina for the time being, where you will not feel yourself existing in a disadvantaged—if still entirely *respectable*—position.

I was relieved, if saddened, to hear her words, and I could not deny the delicacy with which she considered my predicament and rendered her opinion. I arranged to stay two more days, in case there is any news coming to me from Philadelphia, but meanwhile I paid the bill in full and packed the few things I brought with me, in anticipation of departing Memphis. If there is no news forthcoming and if Achilles does not appear on Mrs. Whiteside's doorstep by Thursday next, Mother, I will take the Friday morning cars to Atlanta and stay over, changing to the SCRR and arriving in Charleston the next night. There I plan to spend at least a day or two with Grand-Papa Jones and Nettie before coming home to Cheraw.

You are too decent to say "I warned you this might

happen," so I will say it for you: I should not have rushed to Memphis carrying all my eggs in one fragile basket, just as Achilles should not have defied his father's dying wishes. As he was leading me to the door on the night we went walking, I said it was time I wrote to you and reassured you I was well. He told me that Aunt Mildred was like Priam's daughter Cassandra in the tale of Agamemnon— she saw into the future and warned people truthfully of coming catastrophes, but because Apollo had cursed her no one believed or heeded a word she said.

I hardly know how I found the brashness to say that the gods had not cursed Mother but me, because I was the one who fell in love and lost my reason, along with my last, best hope for happiness.

If he had blushed then, I might have felt that his heart had not yet closed to me, but instead he turned the color of chalk. I cannot give you what you need and deserve, he told me, haltingly. There is too much pain right now. It is everywhere I turn.

As he walked away, I said quietly to myself, *On this point, we agree.*

I went to the gate to watch him go, feeling strongly that my glimpse of his broad back passing under the streetlamp on the corner was the last time I would ever lay eyes on Achilles Fincher Hockaday.

I enclose his envelope, Mother, because I cannot bear to carry it on my person all the way home to Chesterfield County knowing how much anguish it contains. And yet it is so light! If I possess the right to advise you, considering that all your well-intended advice has been wasted on me, I offer this one unequivocal recommendation: burn the damned envelope, unopened, as soon as you read my note. Nothing good can come of it, and much may be lost.

Ever yours,
Roe

PART
THREE

.....

The Cord

.....

AUGUST TO
NOVEMBER,
1892

Le Manoir des Tournesols,

SEGONZAC, CHARENTE,
POITOU-CHARENTES, FRANCE

August 14, 1892

Dear Achey,

Following your brief note in June, summarizing events
since Father's death and notifying me of your departure
from Memphis, I have been the recipient of a distressing
letter from our sister and another, even more distressing
one from Aunt Mildred (more on that later). Helen was in-
dignant on behalf of Roberta's apparent spurning at your
hands. Have you broken our cousin's heart, Achilles? If
nothing else, it sounds as if you bit off more than you had
any intention of chewing . . .

As distressed as Helen sounded on her cousin's account,
I was relieved that she made no mention of your investigation into our parents' private lives. She professes to be
mystified by your precipitous flight to Philadelphia, so I
am assuming you have not divulged your latest discover-
ies to the girls. I think that is wise. Now that I am in possession of those book pages torn from the back of Mother's
diary which you forwarded to Aunt Mildred as you were
leaving Memphis in April, I implore you to keep this information *entre nous*.

I am thankful that you informed me about your investigation prior to the arrival of this material; otherwise I
might still be recovering from the shock of its content.
My imagination will not be parted from it long enough to

focus on anything productive, but returns constantly to
it to feed and embellish its horror. While the events described here are truly nightmarish, the most distressing element of these memoirs may be the stark state of Mother's
isolation on that farm while our father was absent, especially during her *accouchement*, with her most sympathetic
companion in the house being a ghost! I ached for her, and
could not reach into the past to give her comfort.

Mildred asked me not to resent her for conveying the
pages but stated that she simply could not be responsible
for them once she had read them—that they constituted
evidence of a killing that she claimed our mother had
never revealed to her—as well as acts of such depravity
that our aunt felt like a *voyeur* after reading the entries and
could not shake the sensation of being culpable for the
wrongdoing described just by bearing witness to it.

And yet, I cannot find fault with anything you have
done, Brother. It is always better to seek knowledge
than to persist in willful ignorance. Didn't Marcus
Aurelius quote Plato on that score? . . . "No one know-
ingly chooses to live without the truth." Neither one of
us may ever fully comprehend the complex history of our
parents' marriage nor am I certain I will ever understand
your reasons for changing the course of your own life
so radically in response to this history. But had I been in
Holland Creek when Father died, and had he asked me to
burn Mother's diary, I believe I would have acted as you
did. Where we may differ is in how we choose to act in the
aftermath, and whom we involve with our actions.

I wish you luck in your search for the "other" Achilles, while cautioning you to be clear about what you expect from him. If he played a role in the events taking place on the farm in April 1864, as Mother writes he did, he may not thank you for recalling this troubled period of his life or any portion of the time he was enslaved, and he may not acknowledge the ancestry you ascribe to him. Holland Creek, in fact, may be a time and a place he has worked hard these last three decades to forget.

In answer to your question about him and about what I remember from that time, I have no recollection of a negro field hand with blue eyes, but I do have an impression of a compactly built colored man with thick arms and bowed legs, like a wrestler or a groom, someone who smelled comfortingly of horses. He came to the house more frequently than any of the other hands, and seemed to be on familiar terms with Mother. Judging from her diary, I would guess this to be Abner.

I must cut this letter short just as I am making progress—there is a crisis with the largest of the stills and if I do not address this there will be no "bonne chauffes" for my father-in-law's cognac this season nor will my reputation be worth saving by the next one. More to follow—

Your distracted brother,
Charlie

The River

Sunday, very hot. I would take the buggy and go to church today, if it were possible. I have not been able to talk to God in this house. There is no one else I can talk to, except the first Mrs. Hockaday, and she has not made a visitation in weeks. It is not possible for me to go out. I am vomiting several times a day, even without nourishment. I know what the good Presbyterians of Holland Crossroads would whisper to one another if I proved unable to endure two choruses of "O Lamb of God Most Holy" without suffering a bilious attack.

I have not wanted to write in this book for a long time. I supposed that if I didn't commit my memories to paper, there was still a possibility of erasing them. But one's mind isn't like that, of course. It hangs on to everything, like a raccoon with a broken spoon.

(Later)

Charlie cried until I carried him down to the yard to feed the chickens. He is getting too big and I am getting too weak. I sent Cleo away five days ago. I had no choice. She is part of the Parris family; also, her mother has been with the Daniels for more than twenty years. There is too much risk. I cried and Cleo cried and Charlie wailed as if his nurse was being cast into the Lake of Fire and not walking a few miles down the road to Coldwater. I think Cleo knew why I had to do it. She knew when Abner brought her back to the farm on the Monday following the party that something had happened. Nothing was the same. I couldn't hide it. It was too big a secret. It hurt too much. And I couldn't explain why Achilles was gone.

Where has he gone to? He was happy here, wasn't he? You was happy with him, wasn't you, Miss Dia? Has he gone into the woods? Because the runaway-hunters will surely find him there, won't they? He'll be hurt bad. Might we not go looking for him, Miss Dia?

No. No. Let him go. Good riddance. I don't want him back. We don't need him. (Lies and more lies. I ache from all the lies.)

This afternoon I lifted Charlie into the old fig that grows against the south wall of the house and let him pick the early fruits. He stuffed them in his mouth, laughing, but then he picked one with ants and they stung him. He cried as if his heart would break, slobbering with grief, with rage. I held him on the porch and rocked him; I crushed a borage leaf and smoothed it on his fat little hand. Eventually he exhausted himself with weeping and I settled him in his cot for a nap. Then I threw up in a pot.

Bob came to the house to say that he and Winthrop are picking more bushels of peaches every day and they are rotting in the storehouse. There's a woman at the crossroads he can call to come boil up the fruit, put up preserves of the peaches and tomatoes, put up the cucumbers and squash. The figs, too, as they come. You and Master Charles will want that food come winter, he says, eyeing the pot under the table. May he do such?

I nodded, thinking I will have to dig the gold coins out of the lard. It remains to be seen how I will be able to bury my arms up to the elbows in warm grease without spewing a mess in the crock. I closed my eyes thinking he was finished, but he cleared his throat.

The fruit is one thing, he said, and we'll have the crops laid by with one more plowing. But two men cannot gather corn, cut fodder, and set turnips, which comes after. Then the cotton comes on, and the sweet potatoes—

You said two men, I interrupted. Where is Felix?

You gave him a pass to drive the vegetable wagon to Monday market in Spartanburg, Missus. Two weeks ago. I had to ride Sadie there to bring the wagon home. Not seen Felix or the cucumber money. I told you this, Missus.

Mr. Peggotty's dream comes true

July 25, 1864

H E WATCHED ME, SQUINTING, BECAUSE HE COULD NOT TELL if I misunderstood about Felix bolting or if I could be losing my mind. I'm not sure myself, but I think it is the latter. Bob finally said: if Achilles had not run—

Do not speak of Achilles to me, I said, cutting him off. Achilles is not coming back. Bob nodded, rubbing the band of his hat, and I saw in his eyes that he blamed me for his best worker going off. Why shouldn't he? I blame myself.

Then Abner must help in the fields, Missus. And we need another two strong men. Or three, through harvest. If he were mine to deal with it would be the cowhide, laid on hard. But Abner only answers to you, he says.

I swallow hard because all this talk of food has made my stomach heave. Starving seems like a preferable option right now, but I must think of Charlie, even if I no longer believe that the major is returning.

Hire the men. I will pay what their masters require. And I will speak with Abner. He must help in the fields. Of course he must.

WHEN BOB LEFT I carried the pot out to the back porch where Charlie's cot was placed to catch the breeze. I lay down beside him because I felt dizzy, and just as I was drifting off to sleep I felt the life stir inside me for the first time. It felt like champagne bubbles rising in my belly. That's when I wanted to talk to God. But I was too frightened. I was too angry.

When I woke it was dark, Charlie was still sleeping, neither one of us had eaten supper, and I could hear the chickens fretting because I hadn't shut them in the hen house. I must have help.

THIS IS MY PLAN. Aunt Florie wrote to me last week telling me that the servants have been dispersed, with many of the larger families separated who had been at Valois for generations. As I expected, my bid in April for Nerissa did not prevail. Abner returned alone, unfit for any task requiring the full engagement of his will and his faculties. Nerissa was purchased along with several other young females by Alistair Oglesby, my stepmother's brother, and was carried west to a farm he owns outside Abbeville. Now my aunt writes that despite having the company of her cousin at Jessamine, Nerissa has disappointed Mr. Oglesby after less than three months' time through being "sickly" and not up to her duties despite considerable correcting on the part of the overseer's wife, Mrs. Weeks. (Florie explains that Alistair's "decent" overseer left the farm to marry, and that the Weekses, poor whites of no quality come up from Louisiana, are terrorizing the servants in the field and in the house in the mistaken assumption that this will cause them to work harder.) Nerissa has become a special project of Mrs. Weeks, Florie writes, and has been beaten so aggressively by the woman that she now walks with a limp. Florie claims that Oglesby is considering all reasonable offers for the girl.

This morning I wrote back to my aunt, authorizing her to bid as much for Nerissa as that old goat Alistair demands, and to charge me sufficient fee for transporting her as I cannot spare a man, but to send her immediately. I found Abner feeding the livestock and gave him the letter, telling him what message it contains. I explained to him that I will bring his darling to Holland Creek only if he works in the fields like a government mule from now until December, when the last shred of cotton will be plucked off the boll. She will be my Cleo, I told him—she will care for my son and me and she is to stay up at the farmhouse where I will need her night and day from now on. (With that, Abner stole a look at my stomach and I almost laughed to see how quickly he snatched his eyes away again. Perhaps I was a fool to think the men haven't noticed my condition.) She is to stay with me and not in the field house with you, I repeated. Do you understand?

He nodded, beaming. It did me good to see a man so hopeful.

I said, take the letter to the crossroads. When you return, help the men with the peaches. And I turned aside to retch into the straw.

Restoration of mutual confidence between Mr. and Mrs. Micawber

UNDER THE FULL MOON WE SHUCKED CORN, BORROWING FIELD hands from the Byars and the Hambrights. I could not keep out of sight entirely, as there was too much cooking to be done for the hands, but Nerissa had dressed me in a pleated pinafore and a long homespun duster that hides my shape. In truth I have gained so little weight, having been so nauseated through the first four months, that I do not attract much attention.

Charlie was beside himself with excitement and would not sleep, so I let him watch from the porch as the teams went to work on their piles of corn. When Bob's team found the red ear he cheered so loudly I feared he might give himself a nosebleed. After the crib was piled high and locked and dinner had been eaten, the hands walked home, singing and talking. Nerissa put Charlie to bed and she and I worked late into the night scrubbing the rice and meat pots in the cauldron in the yard. She is a quiet girl, often lost in thought, and while she minds Charlie well and is gentle in her dealings with him, he has not formed the bond with her he had with Cleo. In a way, I am proud of him for that. It shows he is not fickle. Despite her brooding, however, she is very suitable as my companion. On her first day at Holland Creek she plucked several pears from the trees and fixed me a concoction of warm water, pear juice, and a pinch of cinnamon. It settled my stomach and allowed me to eat broth that night which stayed down. I told her I was expecting a child and that she must tell no one. She nodded, not asking questions, and told me she could sew proper clothes for me if I could get the cloth. The next day I swapped ten jars of Winthrop's good honey with Mrs. Byars for the homespun and as Nerissa stitched the pinafore together that night she told me softly that Mrs. Byars wove a fair cloth but that she could weave a better one if I would fetch a loom. A letter had arrived from my husband by then, letting me know about the money on deposit at Cowan's, so I bought a used loom from the dry goods man in Laurens and set her up in the side parlor where Charlie and I have slept on a cot since April, Gryffth's loaded revolver under my pillow.

The night of the shucking we were washing pots and talking of this and that. Maybe because of the moonlight falling on our bare arms and Nerissa's soft-eyed face when she turned to me, I felt we could speak intimately. Of private things.

Nerissa, I told her, there was a servant here, a runaway. We named him Achilles. She nodded. Abner told me. Said he run off while Abner was in Valois trying to buy me the first time.

That young man, I said. Maybe twenty-one years old or maybe more, he was born at Valois—did you know?

She stopped scrubbing, looking up at me.

Achilles' mother came to Valois when she was just a girl. She worked in the house as a companion to my mother, Geraldine Fincher, who taught this girl to read and write. My mother was a good teacher, patient and kind. I know because she taught me when I was old enough to learn these things, several years later. But before I was born, this young servant bore a child. When the child was shown to my mother, she ended the teaching, along with the patience and kindness. She required my father to sell mother and son away, which he did, in order to placate his wife. You never saw Achilles, but you know my father, Mr. Quincey. My nickname for Achilles was Blue Eyes.

Nerissa stared.

He was my father's son as sure as I am his daughter.

She waited.

Nerissa, I said finally. Did my father ever . . . ? Did you . . . ?

Here Nerissa dropped her eyes and went back to scrubbing with ferocious vigor. No, Miss Dia. Not him.

We scrubbed in silence. I splashed my pot with a bucket of rinse water and set it on a stump to dry. When I came back to the cauldron she looked in my face, studying it in the blue light of the moon.

What you going to do with it? She pointed her brush at my belly. It's his, ain't it? The mean one? The one that's gone missing?

I dropped my brush to cover my mouth with my hand, but it was too late to prevent the chain of ragged sobs that escaped. Before this I had not wept, not even the day after, but Nerissa's quiet tone had pried open some padlock placed upon my lacerated heart. I can't tell you, I finally bleated. I can't protect you if you know.

1326 Lombard Street,

PHILADELPHIA,
PENNSYLVANIA

September 9, 1892

Dear Charlie,

You are kinder than I deserve in telling me I did right to
pursue my current course. Since finding out that Mother
and Father concealed their true lives, suppressing tales
of defilement, tragic loss and, most critically, redemptive
passion—tales that would have sold briskly on ancient
street corners had their stories been penned by Homer or
Apollodorus—I have been forced to recalibrate my own
life. In doing so, I am trying to weight the scales with
more substance and a significant context. To that end, I
broke off what had evolved into a complicated progression
of affairs with dear Roe after arriving at a stage requiring
either culmination or termination, neither of which I was
willing to effect. I daresay I deserve my aunt's and Helen's
harshest recriminations (Roberta will not communicate—
she has sent my letters back, unopened). I loathed causing
my lovely cousin pain, especially as I cannot fully understand why I was romancing her, and when I am feeling
very critical of the facile young know-it-all I used to be,
I ascribe the basest motives to him, suspecting that he
pursued Miss Jones because she is winsome, highly intelligent, and because she indicated through her rapt attention
to discourse that every word out of his mouth was sub-
lime. Of critical importance is the fact, only understood

in retrospect, that Roberta was tacitly pledged to another man, which had the effect of simultaneously incapacitating this callow idiot's normal restraint and sharpening his competitive instinct. On days I am more inclined to give myself the benefit of the doubt, I perceive that I had disastrously poised myself for making a lifelong commitment to an exemplary woman when I was only a partially developed man—unchallenged by life and almost wholly ignorant of its realities. Mother's diary changed that, along with the other incendiary contents of her trunk, in an intervention that some might call a stroke of luck for such an exceptionally fine woman as Roberta is, but what I call Fate, Destiny. The three Moirai spin and twist the threads of our lives in directions we could not have imagined. Do you remember what Mother used to say? *Life is all about the leaps.* I tell you as I stood on the platform in Memphis carrying nothing but my mother's *David Copperfield* and my grandfather's watch, and as I watched the train that I was due to board steam into the station, I felt a desperate compulsion to leap aboard while the cars were still in motion. That is how impatient I was to arrive in Pennsylvania and commence my search for Achilles.

I cannot say exactly what I was hoping to achieve if I was successful in my quest. Mother's final diary entries make it clear who "fathered" the baby in the spring of 1864, but they do not account for the newborn's death in the winter of '65. Did I expect Achilles to tell me? Did I hope for him to inform me about Mother's state of mind when he departed Holland Creek on that awful April morning? Or did I think he could give me intelligence

about my grandfather, Quincey Valois (his father, by
Mother's reckoning), or the circumstances of his own cre-
ation? No one with a healthy outlook would advise me to
rake up the sordid backgrounds of these and other events
concerning our family and yet I believe that is exactly
what Placidia meant for me to do by preserving the
Dickens. I have come to view the book as my peculiar
birthright from her.

My search for the "other" Achilles involved fruitless
weeks of riding omnibuses and plodding up and down
the streets of Philadelphia to inquire for him at small
newspapers and trade magazines. He lacked a cognomen
when he escaped the Confederacy, so, like a code-cracker,
I was forced to experiment with options, looking for
Achilles Hockaday (so far, I am the only creature so
named), Achilles Fincher, Achilles Valois, Achilles
Holland, and so on. After spending one sweltering July
day on the streets I was so knackered I almost didn't climb
the stairs to the remaining office on my list, but pushed
myself to do so. When I made it to the fourth floor and
collapsed in a chair the young colored woman sitting behind the typewriter asked me coolly if she could help me
with something and I answered without really thinking,
"A glass of water would be appreciated." The temperature
dropped to subzero. "I am not a secretary, if that's what
you're assuming, and I am most certainly not a servant. I
write stories for the *Clarion*." And she went back to typing.

My Southern manners rescued me. I caught my breath,
walked downstairs, fetched two root beers from the corner drugstore, and carried them back to the *Clarion* office,

presenting her with one of the bottles. She gave me a second appraisal, drank her root beer, and asked me where in Dixie I hailed from, because "they don't grow accents like that in Pennsylvania." When I told her I was on the faculty of a college in Memphis, Tennessee, her estimation of me seemed to improve marginally, for she told me that she was from Memphis, too. What's your business here? she asked. I explained that I was searching for a man who had made his way out of South Carolina during the war, who had meant a great deal to my dead mother, and whose experiences I wanted to know more about. With this information the lady journalist became intrigued, if a bit suspicious. (I had become familiar with suspicion by now, and had even been ejected from one hole-in-the-wall newsletter office on 12th Street with the accusation that I was a bill collector.) What's his name, she asked, and when I explained that I didn't know his surname but in my mother's time he had gone by the name of Achilles, which was my name, too, her expression altered to one of extreme attentiveness. She asked, didn't you say this person publishes a newspaper?

He did so fifteen years ago, I answered. Aside from one communication near the end of the war, that was the first and last letter he wrote to my mother.

He may no longer be a newspaperman, she said. Come with me.

She swept up her hat, locked the office, and carried me off down the street, four or five blocks further south. As we trudged up the stairs of the narrow building on Lombard Street, she pointed to the sign on the staircase announcing VIRGIL ACHILLES, ATTORNEY-AT-LAW.

SPECIALIZING IN CONTRACT LAW, PROPERTY TRANSAC-
TIONS AND TENANT'S RIGHTS.

Once in the small office, this assertive young lady told
me to wait in the one chair provided in the vestibule while
she knocked and entered the room sectioned off with a
pebbled-glass partition. I heard dialogue behind the glass,
which became animated at one point before subsiding
into murmurs. After an uncomfortable length of time,
the journalist emerged, facing me with an expression that
while not entirely encouraging, hinted at a small triumph
of will. I have to get back to the office, she told me. He
will see you—go in.

Charles, you cannot imagine with what trepidation and
anticipation I entered that little room. I flattered myself
that I was something like Aeneas, clutching the golden
bough (in this case, golden pocket watch) as I climbed
into Charon's ferryboat to make the crossing to the underworld. Would I meet Anchises, my blood relation, on
the other side of the Acheron, and would we look down
on our descendants, waiting by the river to be born into
the new world that awaits them? Or would I be lost in
the Fields of Mourning, where the judge of souls passes
sentence on those who have caused suffering or have persisted in ignorance and folly? As I stood on that threshold,
I was reminded of Aunt Mildred's exhortations to leave all
stones unturned, and heard the admonitory passage from
The Aeneid I had so lately taught my pupils: "All night
long, all day, the doors of dark Hades stand open, / But to
retrace the path, to come up to the sweet air of Heaven, /
That is labor indeed."

Rather than tell you all that was expressed and experienced when I pushed open the door and sat down opposite my Fincher "uncle," let me tell you that we have met several times since that initial interview, with most of these sessions being conducted peripatetically out of doors, as Achilles confided he cannot bear to be confined for long in small places due to a site he referenced obliquely as "the Armory" and which I recall Mother mentioning in her diary. In other words, he only keeps the office on Lombard for conferences with clients. As soon as it had been established that he was the Achilles I sought (and he was shocked, happily so, to discover that Mother and Father had given their firstborn son the same appellation, while being visibly affected at the news that Placidia was no longer living), we were on our feet striding briskly down the avenue while he smoked and talked and studied me sidelong. So while we are not exactly friends, we are more than strangers, and I am confident we shall eventually define the propinquitous connection that binds us. And when we do, I hope he will allow me to sit down!

Let me assure you that this man is unmistakably cognate with myself and our sisters. I can say that with certainty because when I walked in the door and looked at him coming around his desk to greet me formally, I hallucinated that I was in the presence of Helen some decades hence, if Helen-of-the-future were dressed for a role in one of Shakespeare's comedies of gender-switching. In this case, the effect has been amplified by the defining element of race. He has her confident posture, her narrow hands, her densely blue eyes, as mentioned, with a thin scar spanning his right cheekbone that serves to underscore this anomaly. We shall have to stop calling them Helen's eyes from now on, or Achilles' eyes, or the eyes of their common ancestor, Quincey Fincher. Clearly, they are the bloodline marker of some Plantagenet plotter whose talent for coming out on top over generations of fortuitous couplings ensures a clear gaze and an independent will sharpened by the rules of survival. Virgil Achilles is the inheritor of both.

By the bye, he told me some astonishing things about Miss Alma Jefferies, the young woman who brought about our meeting. I was so overwhelmed at the prospect of ending my quest for the Holy Grail that afternoon that I forgot to ask the lady her name before she left us, but he knows her well. By the time she was twenty-one she had developed a reputation for herself in Memphis as a journalist for some of the freedman papers (and I was embarrassed to admit that I had never read any of them, despite my living there since '88). Then, in March of this year, three colored businessmen were lynched in our fair city. I think I wrote you about the matter at the time, did I not? The mainstream papers gave it short shrift, accusing the negroes of firing on town deputies, but Achilles pointed out that the deputies went en masse to the store owned by one of the darker citizens while two of his friends were helping him in the store, and that these deputies were dressed in civilian clothes, not identifying themselves as lawmen. They wasted no time in threatening the colored men, as their popular store was impacting the profits of a white-owned business across the street. In the ensuing scuffle, three of the deputies were shot. After the three imprisoned negroes were killed by a mob, Miss Jefferies wrote a pamphlet: a kind of causal analysis on this lynching in particular and what conclusions it supports about lynching in general. I took the liberty of borrowing the pamphlet from Achilles and found it singularly edifying; she theorizes that the common reason ascribed to the lynching of colored men in Southern states, that of sexual assault, can often be disproven in specific cases. She argues that the actual reasons for the lynchings are much more often economic and political in nature—due to the threat posed by negro-owned businesses and to political gains made by their race. Apparently Miss Jefferies received so many death threats when the analysis was published that she was forced to flee Memphis in the middle of the night, during which time the office of her publisher was trashed and burned. She has told me since (for I have called on her occasionally) that she does not believe it safe or proper for any colored person to live in a Southern state, so long as the Fourteenth Amendment, ratified over twenty years ago, continues to be detached from full rights under the law.

You will think I digress, dear brother, and you may be right, but in fact during my time in Pennsylvania I have been giving a great deal of thought to my future and to our legacy as a family. I hope I will not shock you when I tell you that I am planning to engage Virgil Achilles' legal services; it seems especially fitting considering my objective. I intend to take the necessary steps to expel Carthene Oglesby once and for all from Valois. Achilles

believes there are good legal grounds, as Carthene ceased
paying all charges on the property years ago and made
changes that amount to "voluntary waste." (A colleague
of Achilles in Columbia will take our brief and argue the
case before the judge there, as only white attorneys prevail
in our home state, where justice has never been blind.)
Then I plan to sell the estate: every sterling gravy ladle,
Waterford chandelier, and ruined slave cabin on the two
hundred acres remaining. There is no sacred honor there
worth safeguarding.

As to the fate of our own homestead: I know Father was
disappointed that neither one of his sons desired to stay
at Holland Creek, devoting our lives to it as did he and
Mother. In light of what occurred there, as documented in
the diary with pitiless clarity, I see now that our parents'
attachment to the farm was likely predicated on mutual
defiance of the Fates rather than any affection for the place
or for the ceaseless toil it required. As strong-willed as they
were, they must have felt compelled to reclaim their future
lives from the blighted shambles of their past; the only way
to do that was to make a stand at Holland Creek. Before
Father died, I assured him that I would keep the farm in
the family as long as I possibly could, but he could see for
himself that with cotton selling for less per pound than it
did the year he returned from the war, the Southern farmer
is at actual risk of extinction. He was lucky—or blessed
with great foresight—to have shifted that role largely to his
tenants over the years and to have capitalized instead on his
talent for breeding fast horses, or we all may have followed
our neighbors into Uncle Floyd's textile mills by now.

Despite the depressed market for farmland, I am hopeful that with the proceeds from the sale of Valois I may be able to improve the lives of my sisters to some small degree and find some work for myself that will contribute to the peaceful coexistence of future generations of our countrymen. Millie longs to follow her physician-mentor to Asia for six months once she finishes her training at the hospital, to serve in a clinic where the good doctor is pioneering treatments for cholera, while Helen, who was being wooed by droves of local boys when I was home during Father's illness, confided in me that she has given the nod to Dr. Gordon's eldest grandson. He owns a profitable timber concern near Glenn Springs and she will be well cared for. During a touchingly earnest dialogue with my fair sister, she assured me that one of the conditions of her engagement to Lem Gordon is that they make their home at Holland Creek for half of every year until Flora marries, and that our younger sister live with them the other half at Glenn Springs (if Flora can bear to be separated from the horses that long). Meanwhile, Winthrop's son, James, has expressed an interest in managing the home place until Flora is old enough to shoulder it or until Helen and her future husband step in to make these decisions; Father relied upon James heavily, so I feel comfortable in agreeing to this arrangement. I should like to help him make much-needed repairs to the stables and improve conditions for the tenants, if I can.

I know you are doing well with Martine's father in the cognac trade, and I also once thought myself well set up at the college, but all that has changed. I wrote to the dean,

resigning my position, and I am going to try my hand at
this and that in Philadelphia while looking at how best to
establish a small press in the city for publications promot-
ing social justice. Miss Jefferies has promised to help.

I can be maddening, I realize, the way I go around and
around a topic. What you are expecting me to tell you is
this: what has Achilles said in response to the events documented in our mother's diary?

He says every word she has written is true.

He says, Don't go out to the shoals to verify remains
that were likely swept away years ago: let sleeping dogs
lie, and that dog's safely chained in Hell, at any rate.

He says he never knew there was a baby, and is sorry
for the poor soul, and for the considerable suffering that
child's birth and death must have caused Mrs. Hockaday.

He said: So your mother put down in writing what took
place at that farm?

I tried to answer but couldn't speak. God help me
Charlie, I nearly burst into tears in front of the man.
He was quiet, letting me gather myself. Then he said, I
wouldn't have left her that night, but she said it had to be.
She was strong, your mother. They shall mount up with
wings as eagles. Isaiah.

He said that many times he expected to be caught and
slapped back in chains or killed on his ten-week-long run
through Georgia and the mountains beyond after leaving
Holland County, and that he had a hell of a time avoiding starvation. The only thing that kept him sane in the
long days while he was forced to hide in canebrakes, in
deep woods, and in the barns of sympathetic Unionists,

was the book Miss Placidia gave him, the first one he ever possessed. He said it told the story of Aeneas, who fled the sacked city of Troy and faced many trials on his journeys around the ancient world, fulfilling his destiny at last by conquering the Latins and founding the Roman empire. He puzzled over that book and worked its verses through and through until he slowly unlocked their meaning and their beauty.

Is that what kept you safe as you journeyed north? I asked him once we'd departed the office and were tramping the busy streets of Philadelphia. Was that book your golden bough?

Achilles halted our march. He planted his feet on the pavement and gripped me by the shoulders to look into my face. "But you know that, Brother," he said to me, his eyes flashing fire. "It was *righteousness* I carried!"

Affectionately,
Achilles

P.S. In discussing the events at Holland Creek, Achilles also said to me, Can't you ask your brother Charlie what he remembers from that time? He was young, but he was also very watchful.

My child-wife's old companion

Here I will write down what occurred on the night of April 15 and the predawn hours of April 16 in this year, 1864. I would not for the world share this of my own volition, but I worry for my servants' sake, if I should die giving birth to this child and evidence comes to light which cannot be explained by anyone living. Achilles is out of harm's way—I had a letter from him in October, not trusted to Cowan's post office but passed along to me through the hands of many servants on many farms—but no one must know his location until the war ends and our country's peculiar institution ends with it. He is the only person who knows this story, who lived it with me.

I will always regret not staying in Laurens that night. I had to follow my own headstrong inclinations, of course, and I let myself be too easily provoked into fleeing my stepsister's dinner party. I paid dearly for my pride. After sitting up to write in Dickens, and burning two candles in the process, I finally lay down in our quiet, empty farmhouse and slept. I was startled awake by a sound that was out of place: that of a key turning the lock on my bedroom door. I only had time to call "Gryffth?" before a man leaped on me as if he were jumping from the window of a burning house, knocking the breath out of me so fully that I could not shout. The darkness was complete—I could not see the man and he did not speak. We battled wordlessly with an intensity so grim it is suffocating to relive. He tore away every layer of clothing and bedding that stood between us while his knees pushed my legs apart and pinned me. I used my hands and nails and teeth and feet to claw and kick. Let this be known: no woman could have exerted herself more in resisting such an attack, not if she were lying in an open grave, fending off the dirt heaped upon her by the monster who aimed to bury her alive. I fought and I drew blood, but I was not as strong as the man bent on assaulting me, and when I gathered my breath again and prepared to call out, he punched me in the abdomen so violently I briefly lost consciousness. Thus his advantage was gained.

And who was I to call? Abner was gone to Valois. Cleo and Charlie were in Laurens with her mother. Bob, Achilles, and Felix were sleeping in the field hands' house, far across the ridge. When it dawned on me that I would be subjected to the ultimate violation, that the attacker was going to take what he sought from me with brutal energy and satisfaction, I told myself: you can survive this violation, Placidia, but you cannot let him kill you. You are young and you must live through this. You will not let him take it all.

That is why I did what he required, for how long I don't know. When he was sated the first time and loosened his hand from around my throat, he said with a little laugh, *Not missing your husband now, I reckon*. I recognized the voice, of course. It was Nolan Oglesby. He smelled of tobacco and horseflesh; his sweat was rank with alcohol. I was too surprised to answer him, but at the same time I told myself I was an idiot not to have seen how inevitable this was. He struck me, yelling, Say it! Then I understood I was to act from his script, speaking as he prompted me.

I mostly played my part, calling him "Master" when he forced me and assenting when asked if I desired still more painful forms of degradation. There were other things I was required to speak aloud, things involving my husband's name, most of them so filthy that I could not shape my tongue to express them, though I was pummeled for my disobedience.

I am the bearer of
evil tidings

At some point—it could have been ten minutes or ten hours into the nightmare—I felt his body soften slightly where he sprawled across me. His breath followed suit, descending into a rhythm of glottal slurps and sighs. He was dozing. I endeavored to slide out from under him in increments, shifting to the side of the bed nearest the window in the desperate hope of flinging myself out of it onto the porch roof, but at one point during the encounter he had tied my wrists together with a piece of baling rope, and it limited my movements. Just as I liberated all but one leg from his crushing bulk, he jerked awake, grabbing me by the hair. I managed to scream before he pulled me backwards on the bed and hooked an arm around my throat, choking off my breath. My face was pointed towards the door when he mounted me again. The door crashed open on its hinges and I howled for mercy, so confused and ravaged at that moment that I thought it was the Devil come to drag us both to Hell.

There was a fire-flash, a shout, and the smell of gunpowder coiling from the doorway. I held my breath, not knowing who had fired the gun or if I had been shot. Slowly, the weight above me shifted to one side. Then it toppled. I lay on my stomach, too frightened to breathe. The dark figure separated from the shadow of the doorway and stepped forward, setting my husband's revolver on the floor before me.

Miss Dia? he asked. Are you hurt bad?

It was Achilles. In Abner's absence he had slept in the hay mow, keeping watch on the horses and the mule. Nolan Oglesby had awakened him galloping up to the barn and leading his big horse into a stall. Because Oglesby was a stranger to Holland Creek, never having visited while Achilles lived there, and because the man acted with such particular stealth, hushing Centurion as the horse stamped and fussed in the unfamiliar barn, Achilles grew suspicious. His apprehension grew when he followed Nolan to the house and watched him slip a piece of meat to Gopher, huddled under the porch. She licked his hand, recognizing him as a Parris household regular. Then Nolan climbed the stairs and unlocked the door with a ring of keys he produced from his pocket, but also in the stealthiest manner possible, taking care to make no noise and lighting no candle when he went inside.

Achilles had peered through the porch window, waiting for some sign of assurance from me. It was not his place to question what the masters did—he had learned this from other white people on other farms. But instead of a lamp being lit upstairs, or my gowned figure greeting Nolan at the bedroom door, the stranger unlocked the door and slipped carefully into my darkened room. It was clear what he was about.

That's when I went to the larder to fetch the major's revolver, Achilles told me later. But it was in pieces on the table. You meant to clean it—

—But left it for after the party . . . I finished, so dismayed I broke off, weeping.

Achilles had assembled the Colt and loaded the paper cartridges with shaking hands. All the while, the thuds and stifled screams of our struggle bore down on him from the room above and made his labor seem hopelessly slow.

When it was finally over and we were readying Centurion, creek mud still clinging to our hands and bodies, Achilles told me he had learned guns from Ben Wilkerson. He said, They let me hunt with him, from the time he was young. I was supposed to go into the regiment with Ben, but the missus couldn't spare me once Master Sam was killed. I sometimes think I could have kept that boy alive.

And where would I be if you'd gone to war with Ben Wilkerson? I asked. That question did not require an answer.

But I have jumped too far ahead in the narrative. The only thing resolved when Achilles burst into the bedroom was that Nolan Oglesby was shot in the ribcage and collapsed across the bolster. When I recognized Achilles I crawled towards him off the bed, trying to speak but hearing my teeth chatter in my head, instead. He raised me to my feet just as Nolan clawed himself upright against the headboard. I dove to retrieve the revolver from the floor. As Oglesby saw me point the barrel at his head and heard me cock the hammer he shouted, *Drop it, you damned c____t!* and the gun fired. I missed him with the first shot, the ball going high. I did not miss the second shot, or the third. I stopped firing when the fourth ball went through my stepbrother's left eye, spraying the wall with scarlet plumes.

I lowered the Colt and looked for Achilles through the smoke. He was standing to my side and behind me, using his sleeve to shield his face. Looking down at myself, my feet spread wide to absorb the recoil, I realized I was as naked as Eve, wearing only my attacker's blood and a fair bit of my own.

The Emigrants

I'M NOT CERTAIN HOW WE CAME UP WITH A WORKABLE PLAN
in the few hours of darkness that remained, considering how
deeply shaken I was, and considering that a man's body lay in
my bed, shot to ribbons. Achilles found me some clothing and a
thick wool shawl and I wrapped myself tightly until the shaking
subsided. He walked down to the field house to meet the men
coming up in response to the revolver's blasts, telling them the
missus had been firing at a rat and now, all was well. The rat was
dead. I boiled water and made coffee, which the two of us drank
scalding-hot, sitting on the bottom step of the stairs. We talked
our way clear to the only workable solution.

It did not matter how vile Nolan Oglesby's actions were—
there was no defense for a negro shooting a white man. If I took
the blame for killing Nolan, charging rape, it would be my word
against the Oglesby family's influence and their high standing
in Charleston society, no matter how many bruises I bared. And
as for that, with Charlie to protect, I could not risk exposing my
reputation in a courtroom. Oglesby would have to disappear,
and Achilles must flee for his life.

Achilles argued against the latter plan, shaking his head when
I told him how dangerous it would be for him to stay here now,
especially if they came looking at the farm for Oglesby based on
what Nolan might have told someone in Laurens, suspecting that
he met a foul end at Holland Creek. Achilles said what happened

tonight showed that it wasn't safe here for me, nor for Charlie. But I did my best to persuade him, knowing that if he stayed, he would hang. Go north, I said. Go breathe free air in a free state. You'll have to skirt horse thieves, patrollers, and Confederates on the march, but you won't have to stay in Holland County one day longer as a slave.

THERE WASN'T ANY MORE time for argument, or for sadness. (How much more sadness could I have felt, that night?) We put Nolan's body in a wheelbarrow and rolled it to a spot several hundred yards downstream, where the creek bed widens for a plateau of limestone shoals. Here the water, slowed and channeled by the shoals, has carved out shallow caves and indentations in the banks that offer rude sarcophagi. We stripped the corpse—my shooting had obliterated all the distinguishing features of its face—and flung it into one of these ready-made depressions. Working as quickly as we could by starlight, we gathered small boulders, gravel, and mud and covered Nolan's remains with a permanent cairn, setting brush atop the rocks to finish.

We returned to the barn and searched through the saddlebags on my stepbrother's nervous horse, finding food and water, a change of clothes, maps, a pearl-handled pistol that looked as if it had once been part of a dueling set, and a small bag of gold coins. (Despite being a vocal champion of the cause, Nolan had clearly appreciated the worthlessness of Confederate currency.) There was also a framed ambrotype of Miss Hammond, her cheeks tinted pink. Looking at her ringlets and her silly, vapid face, I felt an oddly comforting sense of virtuousness, imagining what we had spared her.

While Achilles fed Centurion and watered him, packing oats for the trip, I returned to the house. In the front room I tore an endpaper from one of the books on my shelf and sat down to write a pass for Achilles in Nolan's name, authorizing my servant to ride my mount to Tennessee on his master's business, carrying money to kinfolk in Athens. I rushed the pass to the barn but reversed course and dashed back to the house, grabbing up the book. Back in the barn I thrust it at Achilles. "This was the prize he won at school. He wrote his name on the inside cover."

Achilles opened the book and read the faded script out loud: "Quincey. Valois. Fincher." He studied my face until his eyes widened with understanding. "Virgil," I explained. "It will be good luck for your journey."

I am shown two
interesting penitents

W E TALKED RAPIDLY AS HE CLIMBED INTO THE SADDLE AND
walked Centurion to the road, knowing it would soon be light.
I told him to avoid the main roads and all troop encampments,
traveling by night as much as possible. He told me that if he
were lucky—and there was no reason to believe that Fortune
would smile on anyone engaged in aiding me—he might make
it as far as the Georgia mountains with Nolan's kit, his posses-
sions, and his gold still packed on the horse. (Achilles tried to
make me keep a portion of the coins but I shrank from them; the
transaction implied in receiving Nolan's money made me sick
to my stomach.) He planned to abandon the horse while still a
good distance from Dahlonega, in case the Oglesbys' overseer
decided to meet Nolan further along than planned. He would do
so where there was a hope of its discovery by secessionist Georgians, people likely to preserve the identifying items on the horse
and to pass them on to rebel authorities. They might even notify
the family.

On foot, Achilles would steal north through the mountains
of North Carolina and Kentucky, where the risk of capture was
diminished, making for Ohio. Once there, by whatever means
possible, he was to send word to me that he had survived. Meanwhile, I would wait to hear how Oglesby's family and fiancée

reacted to his disappearance, and if necessary, I would contrive some story for them about his appearing unexpectedly at the farm this night, intoxicated and belligerent, and how my servants and I had to turn him out, setting him on his journey early.

In the end, we need not have worried. I learned soon enough that Nolan had bolted from Laurens in the middle of the night without a word to anyone (excepting Sukie, I presume—his great admirer), leaving a note in his sister's dressing room asking her to look after Miss Hammond and telling her he was getting an early start to his journey because of how much he detested drawn-out departures. No one in Laurens expressed any great concern, until the letter arrived from his grandparents three weeks later, inquiring why he hadn't yet arrived in Tennessee and complaining that most of the negroes at the mill had already run off and the ones at the farm were becoming quite restive with Union troops so plentiful in the Cumberland. Soon after, word began to filter in from various sources that a dappled gray horse had been found grazing along the Soquee River outside Clarkesville, Georgia, a man's torn frock coat located nearby. Documents tucked in the pocket identified the wearer as a Mr. Nolan Oglesby of Charleston, South Carolina, with relations in Laurens and Athens, Tennessee.

In the weeks after Achilles rode away, I often walked to the shoals where we worked so desperately that night to bury Oglesby, reassuring myself that the man was still pinioned under two hundred pounds of stone—that he hadn't climbed out of the creek to torment me with new atrocities. But of course, he didn't need to. The child he planted inside me will serve that function.

Before the night ended I built a fire in the hog-scalding pit and burned the bolster, Aunt Florie's blood-soaked quilt, and the clothes we stripped from the body. The key-ring which we found in Nolan's pocket, the one Sukie kept tied around her waist at Holland Creek, went down the hole in the privy along with the image of my rapist's sweetheart.

Later, I scrubbed gore off the bedroom walls as the violet light of dawn stole over my hands and arms, questioning why Nolan hated me enough to do what he did. I thought of Floyd and Agnes's wedding at Valois, how my stepbrother had scandalized the guests by "coming it over" our servant girls, and how the major had taken him outside to knock some sense into him since no one in Nolan's family saw fit to do so. That could have caused a measure of resentment in the man, I reasoned, but it didn't adequately explain a crime as cruelly violent as the one he inflicted on me. This thought led dangerously to another as I sponged my body clean in the laundry tub: wondering how Achilles was conceived, and how my father could have justified his coupling with a servant girl who hadn't possessed the right to refuse. I moved from shock to fury to madness that night, trying to understand.

One woman losing her sanctity or even her sanity is insignificant when compared to the butcheries committed on both sides in this shameful war. So much blood has been spilled that redemption may be out of reach, in the end. Maybe all we can hope for is to be so exhausted by hate that we settle for the ceremonies of reconciliation.

But I see that the great enemy in this battle is not the abolitionist, the Yankee soldier with his repeating-gun and well-made boots, or the negro who drops his work and runs towards the first scrap of blue cloth he spies between the trees. Our enemy is Nolan Oglesby and all the people like him, who never question their motives or doubt their desires. They are put on this earth to cause misery, because what they take so freely for themselves comes always at great cost to others.

Le Manoir des Tournesols,

SEGONZAC, CHARENTE,
POITOU-CHARENTES, FRANCE

October 10, 1892

Dear Achey,

These are astonishing developments you relate. I don't
know what to say about your plans, except to agree that
it is a new world, and we should be ready for new ways
of working, as well as loving. (And Roberta will recover.
She is leaving for Italy with a school friend, according to
Helen—the Jones shipbuilding fortune will sustain her
for now.)

Your postscript gave me food for thought. In fact, ever
since I received the diary entries from Aunt Mildred my
present existence has been subsumed by memories of a
much earlier one, distracting me to a degree that my family and the workers find irritating. I have been trying to
reassemble these memories—if they can rightly claim
provenance as such—in some kind of intelligible order,
which they resist. On one level, I recall very little from
that time, because I was slow to talk and lived in a world
without language. That world, however, was rich in im-
pressions and sensitive to shifts in emotional temperature
and intensity. I was like a little planet, or a moon, orbiting
around the greater masses of the grown-ups, eclipsed by
their shadows and heated by their brilliance, always attached and dependent.

I have no memory of my first mother, Janet. I would

call her my "true" mother, but that seems disloyal to the mother who raised me and loved me well. That mother, *your* mother, was resurrected with painful vividness in this memoir. In her determination to conserve paper, especially in her final entries, the handwriting is so cramped and the ink-free space so limited that deciphering those passages produced a fearful throbbing in my brain, as if the air was being squeezed out of my lungs in order to elevate the words off the pages. Despite the headaches, the distinctive cadence of her writing in these entries evoked her young presence so powerfully for me as I read them that I was reminded of how I used to grasp her skirts and prop myself against her leg in order to feel her voice vibrate through me. Lord knows how she accomplished all the work she did with Charlie the Possum-Boy clinging to her.

One of my earliest memories, if not *the* earliest, rose up to me as I was reading Aunt Mildred's dispatches the first time. I believe this must have occurred in January 1865, shortly before General Sherman marched his triumphant Union army through our state like a comb, raking the bed of secession. I knew nothing about the movements of hostile armies as a child barely three years old; I only remarked it for being a time of crisis, when the adults seemed poised on collective tenterhooks and there was water everywhere. In fact, there had never been so much water: it rained for days and days. I retain an image of standing on a porch or a stair, watching a crate float by with a rooster riding atop it. I was frightened of the water coming into the house and going over my head, but I didn't have language sufficient to express this. I was crying and fretting a lot, as I recall, but Mother didn't respond to my cries.

Frankly, I am gradually becoming aware of a connection, however shadowy, between these long-buried recollections of the farm during the time Mother struggled on her own, and my decision as a young man to get as far away from Holland Creek as I could manage. I never thought about it when I first went traveling, but now, settled in France with a family and a business of my own, it makes sense as an elaborate kind of *contrecoup*, this displacing myself in order to gain some distance on her suffering. And Father's. Their difficult lives. I have been rereading my old copy of *David Copperfield* . . . did you learn it in school? . . . and was struck by these passages in the Chapter "Absences" (LVIII):

> It was a long and gloomy night that gathered on me, haunted by the ghosts of many hopes, of many dear remembrances, many errors, many unavailing sorrows and regrets . . . I passed on farther away, from city to city, seeking I know not what, and trying to leave I know not what behind.

I don't know if this is all the doing of the Moirai, as you define them, Achilles: spinning, measuring out, and severing the threads of our lives. But as I gather up the unraveled string that led me out of my childhood home to a faraway life in Europe, it leads me back towards that terrible winter.

There was a series of colored girls who minded me at
the farm, and it is strange that I don't remember Cleo,
who I was apparently so attached to, while my most particular memories are of a thin, soft-voiced young woman
who limped as she went about her tasks in the house and
who struck me, even as young as I was, as being perpetu-
ally sad.

Reading Mother's diary, I think this must have been
Nerissa, who left before Father returned from prison, but
who was there during the flood I describe. In the midst
of this crisis she kept trying to shush me, softly. I had the
impression that my mother was behind a door, but I was
prevented from going to her. At one point I heard Mother
crying—screaming, really—and I went running from
that hideous sound to the laundry lean-to at the back of
the house. There was a hiding place under the washtub
that was sized just right for me.

At some point, it might have been that same day or the
next, for there was still water all around, I woke on my cot
and realized that I had been left alone in the house. I was
terrified because the water seemed to be rising, and just as
I was about to start screaming in panic the strongly built
negro of whom Nerissa was so fond—this was Abner, as
I described in my last letter—walked through the front
door carrying Mother in his arms. God, I was relieved—
I thought he had fetched her back for my sake. I ran to
both of them and tugged at her but she was icy wet and
didn't answer. Abner said something to reassure me, I
don't know what it was, and I saw that Mother's arms were

clenched around a little bundle. The bundle was making sounds as if a sickly animal were wrapped in her shawl— as if she had saved a kitten from the flood. Abner carried her into the front room and shut me out.

During that day or night I must have fallen asleep in my hiding place with the rain hammering on the lean-to roof, because I woke when I heard my nurse, the Melancholy Girl, come into the laundry. She was talking, whispering to someone, but not to me. She was holding something in her arms, and I thought it was Mother's kitten. It made kitten sounds, more faintly than before: a weak mewing. I crawled out from under the washtub and tried to hang on the edge of the table to see the kitten, but the girl pushed me down with one hand, gently, and lowered the bundle into the washtub with the other. She was washing the kitten, I thought. I wanted to see, but the washtub was too high. This went on as the rain fell on the roof: sad whispering, sad washing, endless water and the kitten's cries. In time, the mewing stopped. All was silent, except for the water lapping in the tub. I don't know what happened after that. The memory ends. Or maybe it was a dream, and not a memory after all.

Fondly,
Charlie

A Stranger calls to see me
and Endpapers

I DID NOT EXPECT TO WRITE AGAIN IN THIS BOOK. I AM DOING so because there is hope now, where there was none before. Today my husband spoke with the county prosecutor and explained to him that he no longer suspects me of killing my newborn child. Whether or not Mr. Moultrie truly believes him, I cannot be sure, but after questioning Gryffth closely and finding him fixed in his resolve not to testify against me, the prosecutor took him along to Judge Abbott and the three of them talked it out. The judge respects my husband's war record mightily. He was reluctant from the outset to allow Major Hockaday to tarnish his good name by dragging private tragedies into public view, and clearly disapproved of Mr. Moultrie's decision to prosecute me. He granted Moultrie's motion for dismissal today and the charges are dropped. There will be no trial.

How it came about is surprisingly simple. Mildred and Baby Roe arrived on the train from Pendleton several days ago, where they have been staying since Cheraw was sacked. Dr. Gordon extended his hospitality to them, inviting them to stay with me in the rooms he leased at the inn beside the courthouse, where he and his sister, Mrs. Strickland, planned to stay while attending the trial. I told Millie that I was wild to retrieve some of my things from the farmhouse before the trial began, particularly my father's watch and his copy of *David Copperfield*, but my husband refused to communicate with me. Pertinacious Millie, with her formidable powers of persuasion, softened the major's heart with an artfully written note, and he agreed by return messenger to allow me back on the property for one hour yesterday. The major would not be there, Millie told me, nor would Charlie, who had been returned to the care of the Byars family.

As soon as the sun rose, I drove the doctor's jump-buggy to the farm. On this brilliant autumn morning the swamp oaks above the pasture were the color of flames. I wanted to revel in the beauty of the day and the fresh wind, smelling of persimmons, but I was too agitated to appreciate such simple pleasures. In July when the magistrate arrived at the farm to arrest me, I had been unprepared. I rushed about the yard snatching wet washing off the line and fretting about Charlie, who was already sobbing at the prospect of being taken to the Byars' farm by a stranger. I was furious with Gryffth for allowing matters to proceed in this heartless way, frightening his son and treating me like a servant deserving of serious correction. I had known this might be the outcome of my silence, but I did not yet understand how much the war had changed the major. Stiffened him. All I had known for certain when I came around the hen house that first evening in July and saw my husband trudging into the yard after lifetimes spent away from us, a borrowed bag in his hand and the shadow of grief on his face, was that he had to be protected at all costs from knowing what had happened in his absence. I did not believe he could survive it.

Because of how many secrets the diary contains by now, I had taken to hiding it in different places in the house where a casual search would be unlikely to turn it up. My favored location was in the loom, which had been quiet since Nerissa departed with Abner earlier that summer. Left woven on the frame was a portion of homespun which was intended to clothe us when cooler weather came. The day before I was taken away, in the hand-width gap left where the warp met the weft and the shuttlecock rested between, I had placed the Dickens for safekeeping. Somehow I had overlooked it in the confusion of being carried off to jail. While confined in the county court-house and then out on bail at Dr. Gordon's house, I fretted that it could not remain hidden for good, and regretted not having burned it.

I pulled the buggy up to the porch at last and stepped down, tying the horse. A few chickens scratched in the yard, but no one was about. (I had given Gopher to the Hambrights shortly after Nolan Oglesby charmed his way past her into my bedroom, and had felt considerably safer once the watchdog was gone.) I moved quickly into the unlocked house, but was rattled to see that Gryffth was in the process of moving the last of his crop of cotton indoors to keep it dry until it could be shipped to the gin. Making room for the cotton, he had stacked most of the furniture out of the way against the walls, and in the weaving room I was shaken to see that he had dismantled the loom. I pushed the drifts of cotton aside and searched the room, but the book was not there, nor could I find it anywhere downstairs.

In the upstairs bedroom that had once been ours, an old carpet rested on the bed ropes that had held the bolster. A camp blanket rolled neatly against the headboard told me that my husband slept here. On the small table pulled up beside the bed were the remains of a candle burned down to a stub, the hard wax pooled on the polished maple. Beside it sat my *David Copperfield*, the pages splayed open.

1326 Lombard Street,

PHILADELPHIA,
PENNSYLVANIA

November 4, 1892

Dear Charlie,

Your extraordinary recollections have kept me awake for days while I work to comprehend the significance of the events you describe during the flood of '65.

I discovered fairly quickly that my comrade here in Philadelphia formed a habit of sleeping very little in the years since he was young, trying to make up for time lost while his life belonged to others, so occasionally we expend our restless energy in one another's company. Mr. Achilles holds membership in a small club for colored professionals in this city, mostly alumni from the college where he studied law, and he has hosted me there on several occasions in a comfortable lounge where cigars and spirits are available through the night—even fortifying plates of liver and onions, if discussions are prolonged. You know I am a skeptic of the first order and have never been one for table-rapping and that sort of flummery, so don't think me too soft-headed if I tell you that on one of these evenings recently, while we were comfortably ensconced beside the fire with our drinks at hand and only the soft hissing of the flames underscoring our conversation, I distinctly felt Mother's presence in the room with me. I had not been thinking of her at that moment and I had not conjured her so specifically for many years: as

a warm breath, a scent, and an attentive, watchful intelligence. I was not frightened, only grateful to whatever
higher power or consciousness permitted the visitation.

Later, when I was back at my own lodgings and unable
to sleep, it occurred to me that this was one of the reasons
why she hadn't burned the diary. She had hoped—perhaps,
foreseen—that someday I would have no choice but to
go looking for my darker kinsman, and because of that
salvaged connection, I would choose a different path for
myself, a bolder direction. She must have known that such
a path wasn't possible while she lived—that it would have
to wait for another time, in a better world. I have to believe that world is possible.

But here is why I am writing: Achilles said something
last night while we were conferring on the case regarding Valois—something that lodged in my brain and will
not cease plucking at my attention. I asked the man why
he never married—marriage being an institution I am
alternately drawn to and alarmed to contemplate. He told
me very candidly that his bachelorhood would probably
be the main regret in his life, once he neared the end and
was making some sort of final accounting, but that the
years of being someone else's property while young had
inured him to all legally binding compacts. He added that
in his profession he hadn't seen a sufficient number of
happy marriages to determine if matrimony was worth the
gamble.

Without thinking I said, my parents' marriage. That
was good.

He considered this soberly for a moment before saying,

I know your mother yearned for your father's return. And not out of any weakness, but because she seemed to have faith in what they could build together, if they lived through the war. But even then, the odds were against them.

And yet, here I am, I answered, feeling a bit foolish. My sisters and I. Isn't that proof that they beat the odds?

Yes, he said, drawing on his cigar. I reckon that's plenty. But he didn't sound convinced.

It's a question that won't leave me, now that I've read Placidia's book. Most people couldn't survive what our parents did. They must have paid a price for that survival, I'm thinking. It's painful to contemplate, but it has deepened my respect for them. My love. And brought them closer into focus—even to the threshold of men's clubs in Philadelphia.

(And don't think me so obtuse that I don't understand why you needed to migrate to another continent in order to thrive—nor why you will likely not return to this one. Forgive me for pulling you back into that shadowy realm of childhood, Charlie: as the firstborn your acutely privileged perspective on the past is causing me to reexamine everything I thought I knew about our lives at Holland Creek and compels me to consult with the Supreme Authority—you!—in analyzing it. Don't forget: I cannot discuss this with anyone else in our family.)

In remembering our parents with the goal of understanding them more completely, I have been revisiting the discomfiting experience of our sister Helen's birth—something I could never put in context, until now, just as I could never understand why mother seemed to detach

from us, at times. I would have been nine years old, that
winter. I have a clear impression of a very cold day, outside and inside. I had finished my chores and went looking
for Mother in the kitchen out back in hopes I could sit by
the hearth while she and Malvinda cooked dinner—while
we waited for you and Father to come up from the stables.
The kitchen, however, was cold as a tomb. The room
smelled of beef tongue but the fire had gone out beneath
the pot. Malvinda was not there; she must have gone to
town with Millie. Mother stood alone at the small window, overlooking the grove of hog plums and the sliver of
creek moving in the canyon. As she stood staring out at
the frost-covered world, she was slowly rubbing her belly.
That's why the scene is still vivid for me all these years
later: her stomach was so large in contrast to her thin
hands and face. It must have been my first realization that
human babies actually grow inside their mothers, like the
foals and calves I had seen being born on the farm. In my
imagination the child stirred beneath her pinafore.

Mama, is there dinner? I asked. She slowly turned her
head to look at me, but it was chilling that she didn't seem
to see me. Or rather, her ice-blue eyes saw me entirely:
not as her son but as a fellow spirit-traveler, trapped in human form. There was a vacancy in her face that frightened
me. An otherness. She turned back to the window. *There
is nothing so wintry as the sight of birds' nests in the bare trees*,
she said. *So empty now.*

The next day or the one after that, Ephraim brought
the carriage from Spartanburg and took Mother away to
Aunt Florie's house on Church Street. She sat holding her

carpet bag and rubbing her belly: a sphinx looking past us into the frozen hills. I was distressed. Millie cried into Malvinda's apron. Mother must have been gone several weeks, for I remember dressing her garden with turkey manure at Father's insistence. I always did so on the first sunny day in March but never without her working alongside me, chopping out the old roots and singing like a bird at the prospect of spring. Without her, the garden and the house remained bleak, and no one sang.

Father, never loquacious at the best of times, became a virtual mute. Until then, whenever he'd withdrawn into one of his "dark" episodes, his temper flaring and his patience wearing thin, Mother had been there to take him aside and soothe him, like Ajax' Phrygian princess. There was the time I was helping Mr. Fowler feed sorghum stalks into the press: before I knew what had happened Father hoisted me off my feet by the back of my collar and set me down ten paces distant. He lit into the poor cropper so severely, can you bear to recall that?—I thought he would beat him flat as a flitter. Mother intervened in time to save Fowler (not the last time she would do so for our tenants), and after assuring the major that all my fingers were intact and I had not been harmed for the sake of a few quarts of molasses, she coaxed him into taking his rifle and his old dog Rose into the woods to hunt. I think he was gone for three days. He always seemed better when he returned from these hunting trips, no longer crushed under the weight of whatever grim fears oppressed him so. But his wife wasn't there that particular winter, and he was descending somewhere out of sight, within himself.

We were sitting in the side parlor eating breakfast by lamplight, just the sound of our forks clinking and the case-clock chiming the hour. Malvinda's skirts swished as she set down plates; Millie prattled at her side. As my big brother you were slavishly admired, Charles, for being strong when you needed to be and for navigating Father's moods without being cowed by them. That morning I felt such a surge of fraternal pride when you set down your fork, looked directly at the major, and said, "Father, isn't it time you fetched Mama home?"

I held my breath while he raised his head to look at you, the cords in his neck tightening and his black eyes shooting sparks. I was ready to spring to your defense, if necessary. But he didn't shout. Or strike. In fact, he didn't say a word. He pushed his chair back from the table, walked to the stables, and hitched the team to the Concord wagon. He rode to the city that morning and next day he arrived home before nightfall with Mother seated beside him, holding Helen in her arms. She looked happy, I remember that. And when he lowered her from the wagon, Father stayed close, letting the groom take charge of the horses. He kept his arm around her waist all the way into the house and afterwards, as if she and the baby might rise into the air like kites if he didn't hold tight. That was the first time I felt pity for Father. He showed me what a fine line divides love from misery. Sometimes, in fact, there's no line at all.

Live well, Brother
Achilles

Endpapers

It is difficult to describe the panic that carried me downstairs and into the yard, once I understood that Gryffth had discovered my diary and sat reading it through the night. I felt certain that the major had not left the farm after all, but I could not say to what end he waited for me. I listened for the ring of an axe from the woods, a braying mule—but there was nothing. What drew me to the barn was not a sound, but a feeling, like a tug on my breastbone. A weak magnet. I stepped in cautiously, blinded by the darkness after so much morning light. I hoped I was not too late. After a moment I made out my husband's form, seated on an overturned milking bucket. His body was turned away from the door, as if he didn't want to see the sun coming over the ridge or the scarlet leaves flashing. For a few awful moments I thought he might be dead. Then his ribs lifted slightly. He breathed.

Because of the work he'd been conducting the previous day, moving the cotton from the barn to the house, he was covered with lint. Lint clung to his dark scalp, his beard, his shaggy eyebrows, his shoulders. I saw what he would look like when he had grown much older, when death finally marked him as her own. The sight plunged into such a deep place in my heart that it stopped my breath. I felt the love, again. Not that it could help me now. He held the Colt in his lap.

How can I live knowing what you have endured, he asked. His rough voice echoed in the barn. He did not look at me when he spoke. How can I live knowing that I let it happen?

How can I live knowing what *you* have endured? I asked him. The answer is: we shall have to learn.

I came a few steps closer and stopped when I could smell his skin again, that scent of fresh-cut cedar. It confirmed he was still Gryffth, still the man who stepped out of the arbor and grabbed my life by the reins. I made sure he saw me in the dusty light, and that he heard me clearly.

Gryffth Hockaday, I said, everything I did was done for us. For what I imagined we could become together, someday. I will let it be your choice to fire that weapon, if you think it can't be made right. But kill us both, if you do. Me, first. Then you. That's the only way it makes sense after all this suffering.

He twisted to look at me as if he had never considered hurting me. It was an idea he had to turn over in his mind, as he turned the revolver in his damaged hand.

Setting my feet in a wider stance, I closed my eyes and tilted my head back until I felt the shaft of sunlight from the hay mow spilling on my shoulders. I waited. There would be noise, I knew. There would be blackness. But then there would be peace.

I heard the bucket clatter. His arms closed over me like wings. He buried his face in my neck and I still don't know which one of us was weeping.

ALL THROUGH THE NIGHT Gryffth clung to me as if I were wreckage holding him up on a frozen sea. In this way, we are bits and pieces of our former selves.

He said he would not leave me for the world, and I believe him. I said I loved him as I ever did, and I hope he believed me. The truth is harder, as the truth often is.

We are no longer blessed with innocence, nor do we deserve to be. Paradise may have been lost, but paradise is a bad bargain. It costs too much. It conceals serpents, and is littered with graves.

I would rather have this: my husband wrapped around me, his breath against my face. The cord, or something like it, sustaining me.

ACKNOWLEDGMENTS

The only thing wanting is the necessary thing,
a great patch of open sky, like this. Always try to keep
a patch of sky above your life.

—MARCEL PROUST,
In Search of Lost Time

I AM GRATEFUL TO THOSE WHO HAVE HELPED ME KEEP THE patch of sky visible above my life, even when writing was constrained by the necessities of making a living or when inspiration was required to wait upon duty. Primary among these are my husband and daughter, who serve as veritable tent poles for that sky, and SUSAN GINSBURG, my stellar agent at Writers House, who has faith (and sky) to spare whenever I run low.

I am also indebted to those who aided with the crafting of this novel:

KATHY PORIES, my excellent editor at Algonquin, whose meticulous process proved so productive for the story and its characters.

STEPHEN SHORT, for generously sharing family stories and documents dating back to the mid-nineteenth century, including a handwritten account of a wealthy planter's goods and chattels auctioned in upstate South Carolina in 1860. The recorded sale of counterpanes, sausage mills, bedsteads, chandeliers, prize bulls, and human beings demonstrates that before the war a strong mule could fetch close to three hundred dollars in the region, while a healthy "servant" ("1 negro woman Isabella") was worth over four times that.

LAURIE WILLIAMSON, for reading, critiquing, and fact-checking early drafts of this book, advising on social etiquette in southern drawing rooms, and driving to Columbia, South Carolina, to attend lectures on the 150th anniversary of Sherman's invasion. She was especially helpful in partaking of a "period-appropriate" luncheon (oyster bread, pressed quail, and strawberry syllabub).

LEONARD PEARSON and VIRGINIA EDWARDS, former librarians at my hometown library in upstate South Carolina, and SUSAN FULTON, current librarian there, for their assistance and companionable presences on the many occasions I worked in the library's History Room. I am also grateful to the patient volunteers at the Gaffney South Carolina Family History Center in the Gaffney Mormon Church who helped me decipher 150-year-old court documents; SUSAN CLOER of the Marlboro County Historical Museums in Bennettsville, South Carolina, who guided me through the museums' collections and extant antebellum structures; and the staff of the Photographic Archives and North Carolina Collection at the Wilson Library, University of North Carolina Chapel Hill, especially the archivist of the Ambrotype Collection.

JULIE TRELSTAD, digital wizard at Writers House, and STACY TESTA, for all their capable assistance.

ABIGAIL THOMAS, for offering words of encouragement in the basement washroom of McEwen Hall, Queens University, at a time when they were sorely needed. They continue to sustain me.

LILY BLAIR RIVERS VAN PATTEN TUTTLE, JD, who is a constant source of inspiration to my work and a wellspring of positive energy in my world. She lent her legal acuity while I was constructing the judicial backdrop for this novel and working to comprehend laws on life-estates (any errors in that regard are my own), offering the kind of unconditional encouragement of which mothers dream but can scarcely hope to deserve.

FREDERICK VAN PATTEN, without whom the blue sky would have vanished long ago. With his ear for the honest word and his long-practiced eye for pivotal dramatic moments he serves as a vital magus of the writing process and an irreplaceable source of emotional sustenance. Thank goodness we boarded that plane together.

AUTHOR'S
NOTES

Holland County, along with the farms and towns it encompasses, is a fictional district. It exists roughly in my imagination at the junction of Spartanburg, Laurens, Union, and Newberry counties in the upstate region of South Carolina.

Memphis Presbyterian College, the college where Achilles Hockaday teaches Classics, is also fictional. In its mission and its curriculum as a private liberal arts institution, it somewhat resembles Southwestern Presbyterian College, which moved to Memphis from Clarksville in 1925 and is now Rhodes College, but it is based geographically on the campus of Christian Brothers University, in midtown Memphis, Tennessee, which was founded in 1871.

Those readers familiar with the struggles of African-Americans to achieve political and social gains post-Reconstruction will no doubt recognize similarities between the character of Miss Alma Jefferies, the reporter for the *Clarion* newspaper in Philadelphia who forms a working friendship with Achilles Hockaday, and Ida B. Wells, the fiery journalist, suffragette, and advocate for social change who was forced to leave Memphis after her outspoken reporting of the lynchings of three black men there in 1892. Miss Wells's record of courageous advocacy in an age marked by racism so pervasive as to be nearly institutionalized is more heroic that a fictional character can aspire to, but Miss Jefferies borrows Miss Wells's spirit, if not her full range of accomplishments.

I have made every effort to be accurate about the troop movements of the 13th SC Infantry Volunteers, their division and corps (the 3rd CSA) and their engagement in battles with Union troops. Any errors I made are my own, and are not the fault of those who advised me on these subjects. At select points in the narrative I employed creative license in a limited fashion where it served the story without rewriting history. In assigning Hockaday to the 13th, for instance, I added an additional major to the regiment rather than eliminate any of the officers who served in that capacity, including Major David R. Duncan, who, like Hockaday, was captured, and Major Joseph L. Wofford, who was forced to resign after being injured at Fredericksburg. Others who held that rank in the 13th were either promoted, killed, or both, as was the case for Col Benjamin Brockman, who is mentioned by Hockaday in one of his letters to Placidia. The colonel died a month after the bloodbath at Spotsylvania, when the wounds he received there turned gangrenous.

SOURCES

I FIRST READ ABOUT ELIZABETH KENNEDY, HER HUSBAND Arthur Kennedy, and their painful legal dealings with one another during the years 1865–66 in *Confederate Tales of Candler and Connected Counties* [Georgia] by Hu Daughtry. While Gryffth and Placidia Hockaday are fictional characters, Daughtry's account of the inquest into Elizabeth Kennedy's concealment of her illegitimate child's birth and death, and of her husband Arthur's bitterness at coming home to a disgraced bride after four years spent fighting for a lost cause, proved inspiring.

In writing this book I have relied on primary source accounts from the period and from the geographic region encompassing the two Carolinas, not just for providing detailed information about the period, but for help crafting authentic voices for the main characters in the narrative. I found three books in particular to be extremely helpful in this regard: Tom Moore Craig's *Upcountry South Carolina Goes to War: Letters of the Anderson, Brockman, and Moore Families 1853–1865*; Bess Beatty's *Alamance: The Holt Family and Industrialization in a North Carolina County 1837–1900*, and

I Belong to South Carolina: South Carolina Slave Narratives, edited by Susanna Ashton.

In crafting a seasonal farm calendar for Placidia Hockaday and a set of wartime experiences for Gryffth, far away in Virginia with the 13th SC Volunteers Regiment (Brockman Guards), I was assisted by the letters of rural Spartanburg County's antebellum families and at least one of their literate servants provided in Craig's collection. These letters document daily life in the Reidville area during the Civil War, a community I have visited several times. The letters also provide firsthand accounts of Confederate military camps, battles, and time spent in army prisons by the local men who fought with the 13th, 3rd, and 5th SC Volunteer regiments.

I was introduced to *Alamance*, Beatty's incisive analysis of a Carolina planter's family turned textile titans, in 2010 while attending a week-long National Endowment for the Humanities Seminar in Elon, North Carolina, "Building the New South." Beatty's book focuses on the divide between wealthy white southerners and poor ones, sketching a profile of the privilege enjoyed by the planter class prior to the Civil War. The most memorable of the primary sources she includes are letters written by young Thomas Holt, heir to the Holt dynasty, self-described in 1850 as "a perfect stud monkey." Holt provides the factual basis for the story I present in the novel of a young Charlestonian who is a guest at a family wedding. Holt's excitement over squiring a young kinswoman to a double wedding in Haw River, followed by celebrations with other eligible young women over the course of three days, evidently inflamed his libido to such a degree that he left his brother's reception in order to visit the slave quarters on his father's plantation. In the process, he dirtied the knees of his pants so badly that he was forced to change his trousers before returning to the party. Holt recounted the event in a letter to a cousin: "I come it over some of their yellow maids the night at Pa's . . . every personed noticed it but I dident care a dam" (45). I am also indebted to young Holt, via Beatty, for a period-appropriate simile describing how he acted on his attraction for a young lady who shared a carriage ride with him ("I tell you I set to her like a pig upon a tater pelin. . .") (44).

Susanna Ashton's collection of South Carolina slave narratives, *I Belong to South Carolina*, cannot be read impassively, as these accounts are memoirs by the survivors of an American holocaust. Especially unforgettable is "Recollections of a Runaway Slave," which was first published in an abolitionist newspaper, *Advocate of Freedom*, in 1838. In this oral history, a Charleston slave recounts his three-month detainment at the infamous "Sugar House," a facility adjacent to the city's jail (so named because that is where slaves were sent by their owners to have their attitudes and dispositions "sweetened"). The narratives in this anthology are also valuable for their authentic record of daily life on large plantations and small farms in the region as the institution of slavery was weakening and finally collapsing in the waning days of the war; I have drawn on them in crafting portraits of relations between "servants" and masters during this period of transition.

For my depiction of the inquest conducted at Holland Creek, I was guided by the style and format found in inquest records from Pickens County, S.C., contained in *A Genealogical Collection of South Carolina Wills and Records, Vol. 1, 1857–1866*, compiled by Pauline Young (Southern Historical Press). I am grateful to the History Room of the upstate South Carolina library, where I did much of my research, for making this volume available.

I read numerous books and published material about General

William Tecumseh Sherman and his decisive march through Georgia, South Carolina, and North Carolina in 1864 and 1865, but one of the most helpful reference works was *Sherman's March* by Burke Davis, published originally by Random House in 1980. Davis's account of this campaign, so devastating to the Southern states in its path and so instrumental in accelerating the war's end, is slim as military histories go, barely three hundred pages, but it conveys the excoriating reality of this bloody conflict. The story Mildred Jones tells Placidia about an acquaintance who was forced to flee Winnsboro, S.C., ahead of Sherman's legions—of Union soldiers burning the Episcopal church there and desecrating the churchyard—is based on Davis's account of Winnsboro's sacking.

General Lee's Army: From Victory to Collapse, by Joseph T. Glatthaar, was also helpful in providing a comprehensive profile and history of the Army of Northern Virginia. Digitalized collections of rosters, battlefield accounts, and troop movements, by the 13th SC in particular and the ANV in general, were greatly appreciated for the range of information they provided. Especially helpful were websites for the 13th South Carolina Infantry Regiment Descendants Association, the 13th South Carolina Infantry Regiment page of *The Civil War in the East*, the 13th South Carolina Infantry Regiment website created by S. Batson, and the National Park Service's sites featuring Civil War battlefields, particularly the site on Gettysburg.

An excellent online source for anyone writing about the Civil War's impact on Southern lives is *Documenting the American South: Primary Resources for the Study of Southern History, Literature, and Culture,* a comprehensive archive of photographs, diaries, oral and audio histories, and other records of events, customs, and ways of life in the South as preserved and digitalized by the University

Library of the University of North Carolina at Chapel Hill. Diaries and letters of women in this collection who represent the collateral damage caused by the Civil War, especially when it was being waged on their own farms and in their homes at great cost to their families, were extremely useful in informing Mrs. Hockaday's experiences. The histories of white and black Carolinians growing up on farms in the latter decades of the 19th century and the disadvantaged years of the 20th, when the South lagged behind the rest of the U.S. socially, politically, and economically, provided valuable insights into the art of self-reliance that was perfected by Placidia's survivors.

The

SECOND
MRS.
HOCKADAY

.....

Voices: A Note from the Author

Questions for Discussion

VOICES:
A NOTE FROM THE
AUTHOR

In the summer of 2014, I was in the library near my home in rural South Carolina. I was doing research for a book I'd been trying to write on and off (mostly off). It can be a hellish experience for a writer when no amount of work on a project pays off in terms of the story taking flight, and that was the case with my draft about a middle-aged woman living on a farm during the Civil War. I seemed unable to locate the nexus of the story, what Turkish novelist Orhan Pamuk so aptly refers to as "the secret center."

On that July day, however, locked in the tiny, stifling History Room, I stumbled across the summary of an 1865 inquest. As soon as I read it, I knew this was a story begging to be told in novel form. A Confederate soldier who had been away from his teenaged wife for four years arrived home at war's end to confront rumors that his bride had become pregnant while he was away. It was alleged that she had given birth to a son who had been killed and buried on their farm. The baby's remains were unearthed, and the angry husband pushed to have his wife indicted for murder.

The young woman refused to speak about the baby or to name the father. She maintained this silence for the rest of her life, even though she and her husband eventually reconciled.

I was electrified by the plight of this young woman and by the extraordinary courage she must have possessed to face this ordeal alone in a war-torn world. I gathered up my things and ran home from the library with the voice of a fictional soldier's wife, the second Mrs. Hockaday, already telling me her story and an entirely new novel taking shape around her voice. The rest of that summer is a blur in my memory. That's because writing this manuscript was the most intensely concentrated, inspiring, and creatively engaging process I have experienced in all my writing years. Writing the first draft of this novel, which I did in a period of twelve to fourteen weeks, was an experience very similar to falling in love: I was unable to eat, sleep, or think productively about anything but the beloved. Pamuk also says that "the task of writing a novel is to imagine a world," and the longer I spent time with Placidia Hockaday—as Holland Creek collapsed around her, the farm besieged by bummers, kidnappers, runaway servants, and slumming Charlestonians, and as her values shifted and she came to see the Confederacy's lost cause for what it was—the more I felt I was closing in on the secret concealed at the heart of her dilemma. It lay in Placidia's experience of the war as a woman, as someone her son Achilles describes long after her death as a lonely girl "whose spirit ruled her life, for good and ill."

I DON'T REMEMBER consciously deciding how the novel would be written. It began writing itself as it wished to be, in the form of linked found pieces: the inquest record, letters to and from the main characters, and the diary that Placidia kept as she struggled on her own at Holland Creek, entries written on the backs of illustrations in her copy of *David Copperfield*. I suspect I was strongly drawn to the epistolary form by the dormant playwright in me. A decade of my life was spent writing and working in regional theater, and I think I wanted to steal some of the theater's intimacy for this novel by allowing the characters' voices to speak directly into the reader's ear without narrative filters. Even a first-person viewpoint was too limiting in this context, because the story extends beyond Placidia's death to include members of the next generation who are strongly affected by her revelations and by the legacy of the blue-eyed man who is her "darker kinsman."

At the center of the novel is the love story of Placidia and Gryffth Hockaday. They enter into their marriage with a recklessness born out of wartime urgency, only to be parted almost immediately. Gryffth's duties as a field officer in the 13th South Carolina regiment keep him far away in Virginia, while back at Holland Creek, Placidia struggles to cope not only with the endless tasks required in running a farm but with the disintegration of an entire society. Like the heroes in the ancient epics, she is rewarded for her journey of sacrifice and struggle with knowledge. But that knowledge comes at a terrible price.

Gryffth pays dearly for his own survival on the bloody fields of Gettysburg and Spotsylvania, with Placidia telling her cousin Mildred that he "won't allow his suffering to have meaning." When he returns, the two of them must find a way to regain trust and rebuild their lives in spite of their damaged hearts. They must also redefine their dependency on and kinship with the enslaved people at Holland Creek, African Americans who are carving out new roles for themselves in the chaotic aftermath of the Civil

War. Placidia and Gryffth must reconcile themselves not merely to a changed marriage, but to a changed world.

WRITING IS HARD, lonely work for the most part. But when it is fueled by inspiration, and when the stories begin falling headlong onto the page like treasures spilling from a buried chest, it is the most purely ecstatic experience most writers are ever likely to experience. That might be why it's so difficult to put a novel to rest once it's finally complete, accepting that the characters you've become so intimately familiar with will have to carry on without you. Crouching beside Placidia in her room at dawn, scrubbing blood off the walls before the servants arrive at her farmhouse, I felt the beauty, the anguish, and the paradoxically fragile power of her existence in my fictional world. For that short time before the sun rose over the ridge, I shared the secret center with her.

QUESTIONS FOR DISCUSSION

1. Why is the story told in documents—letters, inquest reports, and diary entries—rather than a continuous narrative from one point of view? What do you think the writer intended to achieve by using this approach to the story? How does it affect a reader's relationship to the story?

2. Placidia agrees to marry Major Gryffth Hockaday after knowing him for less than a day—a short engagement, even by wartime standards. What do you think motivates her to accept his proposal and exchange the security of her home for an unknown adventure with this man? What does she mean when she says to her cousin Mildred, and, later, to her children, that "life is all about the leaps" (pages 12 and 214)?

3. Discuss the role played in the novel by the ghost of the *first* Mrs. Hockaday. Why do you think she haunts Holland Creek? What does her relationship with Placidia tell you about the *second* Mrs. Hockaday?

4. Before the Civil War, it was customary among white slave-owners to refer to their slaves as "servants" and to give them names derived from Roman literature and history, as well as from the Bible. Why do you think white Southerners were motivated to do this?

5. Placidia seems to have a close relationship with her father, Quincey Valois Fincher, but her perception of him changes when she discovers that he fathered a child with a slave girl while Placidia's mother was alive and allowed that child to be sold away. In light of recent genetic evidence showing that many of our country's founding fathers, including Thomas Jefferson and George Washington, maintained "shadow" families of mixed-race descendants on their plantations, discuss the significance of this part of America's history. How do you think high-society Americans in the eighteenth and nineteenth centuries rationalized the sexual exploitation of enslaved African American women?

6. Without identifying the person who buried her infant's body, Placidia tells the officials conducting the inquest that she asked that person to wrap the newborn in a piece of her knitting and bury him in the first Mrs. Hockaday's sewing box, because she "could not bear for him to go into the next life unaccompanied by any mementoes of loving attachment in this one" (page 79). What does this tell you about Placidia's feelings toward the baby? Discuss what kind of emotional state you believe she was in at the time of the child's death.

7. Many people in Holland Crossroads believe that Placidia murdered her infant son before burying him on the farm, but no one

involved in the case can determine how the baby died or who might have been responsible. Placidia denies harming the baby. What version of events do you believe? How did the child die, and why?

8. Discuss Gryffth Hockaday's state of mind as you interpret it from his letters to Placidia. How do his views on the war appear to change as he survives more and more brutal warfare? How does he view his own responsibility as a field officer to his regiment of infantry soldiers? How does he view his responsibility to Placidia, left alone on the farm?

9. One recurring motif in the novel is the story of Adam and Eve being expelled from Paradise. What elements does Placidia's story share with Eve's? What "fruit" does she eat from the Tree of Knowledge, and how does it change her?

10. At one point in her diary Placidia comments on her stepsister Agnes Oglesby's dislike of her, saying, "I perceived that nothing Agnes valued was held in high regard by me. That was the injury I caused her as well as the leverage I brandished" (page 181). How does this statement characterize the relationship between the two women?

11. Placidia's grown son, Achilles Hockaday, is repeatedly instructed by his father to burn the copy of *David Copperfield* that contains Placidia's wartime diary. However, like Pandora in the Greek myth, Achilles is unable to comply. Discuss Achilles's decision to read his mother's diary. Would you have done the same?

12. Roberta "Roe" Jones, Mildred's daughter, is heartbroken when Achilles Hockaday breaks off his involvement with her and leaves Memphis for Philadelphia. What does Roe mean when she writes that she should have seen this coming, because it was her own *hamartia*—a fatal flaw in her character—that invited this disaster? How do you feel about Achilles's treatment of Roe, and why do you think he was courting her in the first place?

13. Allusions are made in the novel to Virgil's *Aeneid*, which tells the story of Aeneas, a Trojan who survived the sacking of his city by the Greeks. He traveled the ancient world doing battle with his enemies and ventured into the underworld to visit the dead before finally settling in Italy and founding the Roman Empire. The African American Achilles relates strongly to Aeneas, as does his namesake, Achilles Hockaday. Discuss why the two men see themselves in this role. And what is the significance of this passage quoted by Achilles Hockaday: "All night long, all day, the doors of dark Hades stand open, / But to retrace the path, to come up to the sweet air of Heaven, / That is labor indeed" (page 217)?

14. Placidia's final entry in her diary is also the conclusion of the novel. Do her final words and images leave you hopeful? Sad? Enlightened? Conflicted? What do you think she means by the statement "Paradise . . . costs too much" (page 254)?

TASHA THOMAS

SUSAN RIVERS was awarded the Julie Harris Playwriting Award for *Overnight Lows* and the New York Drama League Award for *Under Statements*. She is also the recipient of two playwriting grants from the National Endowment for the Arts. She holds an MFA in fiction writing and lives in South Carolina. *The Second Mrs. Hockaday* is her first novel.

www.susanriverswriter.com